Mirror of My Heart

Laura Weyr

Journey Press
journeypress.com

Vista, California
Journey Press

Journey Press
P.O. Box 1932
Vista, CA 92085

CREDITS
Cover design: Sabrina Watts at Enchanted Ink Studio

First Printing December 2023

ISBN: 978-1-951320-26-3

Published in the United States of America

JourneyPress.com

Note

This book contains scenes of an explicitly sexual nature between two women. All sexual activity in this work is consensual and all sexually active characters are 18 years of age or older.

*For Erica Friedman, whose kind words
about my earliest Sapphic stories
helped me find the confidence to write this one.*

Chapter 1

I was nineteen when I finally realized that I was in love with my stepmother.

I know. I know what you are thinking. But consider: my father, who had the entire kingdom to choose from, chose the most beautiful woman in the land to be his second bride. She was just nineteen and I but seventeen when they married, though she seemed far older, aloof and beautiful and untouchable. It was only much later that I learned how frightened she had been.

But in the beginning, I was prepared to hate her...and for her to hate me.

A few weeks after my seventeenth birthday, I was awoken by my panicked maid with the words, "You are to dress and come and meet your father's new wife."

"New wife?" Confused and sleep-sluggish, I grabbed a fistful of the blankets she was attempting to tug away.

"The king has remarried. You are to come and meet your new stepmother at once."

"He–he *what?*" My initial bewilderment gave way to choking rage as the words sank in.

I had no particular loyalty to my mother, never having known her. Nor did I care about my father's happiness. He'd had little enough care for mine, leaving me in the hands of a wet nurse, a nanny, and eventually a veritable army of tutors as he fought his wars.

But to bring a stranger into my home, one who would surely try to control me, without so much as a by-your-leave, was intolerable. Soon enough he would be gone again, where-upon she would no doubt become my jailer and tormentor.

"I will not go," I snarled childishly, as though a refusal could do anything other than earn my future stepmother's enmity and punishment.

"Th-the king said he will lock you in your room for a month if you do not obey properly," my poor maid stammered out. I knew this to be no idle threat and so, seething, I complied.

I'll never forget my first sight of her. I stepped into the throne room and dropped into a low curtsey, waiting obediently for my father's command to rise. Only then did I dare to look up.

The first thing to catch my eye was her hair. Most people I knew were dark-haired and pale-skinned like myself. Her hair shone in the afternoon sunlight, making the gold jewelry she wore seem dull in comparison. I wondered vaguely if she might be a political match with our northern enemies. But there had been no public wedding, no display of pomp and wealth and reconciliation, just this abrupt return. Perhaps a captive bride, then?

She met my gaze serenely, too self-possessed for one being held against her will. Her eyes were a remarkable shade of blue, brighter than I would have thought possible, and fringed with startlingly dark lashes. She seemed like a lovely porcelain doll, far too beautiful to be real.

"Come closer," she bade me.

She did not smile, but looked me over with a cool, serious expression. "Yes, a lovely young woman," she said. "Skin as white as snow, hair as dark as night, lips as red as blood, just as they say." After a long moment, she nodded as though to herself and said, "I will call you Snow White."

I blinked. "But stepmother, my name is —"

She shook her head, stopping me. "Never give someone

your True name, child."

"But everyone already knows—"

Her eyes turned cold. "Are you arguing with me, Snow White?"

A chill ran down the back of my neck. "N-no, your majesty."

She nodded, the frigid quality fading somewhat from her expression. "You may call me," the smallest of smiles tugged at the corner of her lips as I watched, startled and suddenly unable to look away, "Alcina. There is no need of any other name or title between us."

Curtseying again, I said, "Yes, Alcina."

"Good," she said. There was a moment of something which in a person with less poise I might have called 'hesitation'. When she spoke again, her voice was as even as ever. "I cannot replace your mother," she said. "But perhaps we can be friends."

I stared.

Friends?

I tried to imagine my father saying such a thing—to me, to any child suddenly under his care, to anyone at all—and could not.

This woman would dictate my life going forward. While the servants might hesitate to punish me, allowing me to run wild and do as I pleased, surely she would not. And yet, even as I tried to cling to my anger, I felt it melting away like ice under a hot sun, a new fascination taking root in its place.

This woman, regal and proud and everything a queen should be, wanted to be friends with *me*? The wild princess? The little hellion?

I barely managed to swallow back a laugh. Well, she would learn her mistake soon enough. I always played at being obedient while my father was there, but it wouldn't last. Once she saw what I was really like, she would be rolling her eyes with exasperation and snapping with frustration just like everyone else.

And yet, "I would like that, your majesty," I found myself saying, and meaning it.

I hated the thought of giving up what little freedom I had managed to wrench from my restrictive life. But I couldn't quite hate *her*.

"Good," she repeated, this time in obvious dismissal.

Everyone said that my father was clearly besotted, but it didn't take him long to leave the palace, the call of the battle-field apparently stronger than even the lure of the new beauty in his bed. Alcina was left in charge of the castle, the land, and most importantly as far as I was concerned, me.

I had no idea how to treat her at first. She was cold and proud, her back always stiff, her expression always unperturbed. Standing next to her untouchable beauty made me feel dirty and unkempt in ways that I'd never cared about before.

Soon enough I began challenging her, skipping out on my lessons and running wild. I wondered if she would punish me as my tutors threatened. My maid whispered that Alcina was a witch, and that she would turn me into a toad if I defied her. I responded that I would prefer to live as a toad.

I was called to see Alcina after a particularly messy mishap. I'd been attempting to climb a tree to reach a tempting apple, gleaming and red at the end of a branch. Of course I'd slipped and fallen, my weak and untrained muscles unable to hold me up.

To my surprise, I wasn't brought to the throne room, but

to Alcina's personal chambers. The servants abandoned me in the empty front room, a comfortable space with soft chairs, a fireplace and bright tapestries on the walls. One shelf held a miscellaneous collection of texts. I would have gone to inspect them, but just then Alcina's voice called out, telling me to enter her bedchamber. I did so.

She was sitting in the window seat, a cozy-looking nook filled with cushions. The space received a great deal of light from the surrounding windows. I hadn't known a place like this existed in the castle. She looked far softer, wearing a simple dress and not the heavy gold-encrusted fabric that I had always seen her wearing before. Instead of being bound and arranged as it usually was, her hair was looser, coming free of its single clasp. Lifting her eyes from her book with obvious reluctance, she looked me up and down. Her sigh made me want to sink into the floor.

"What shall I do with you, Snow White?" she asked.

"I don't know," I mumbled, dropping my eyes.

"If you wanted an apple, one of the servants could have gotten it for you," she said. "They have a wonderful invention called a 'ladder' that allows one to reach even the highest branches safely."

I peeked up at her, a little shocked at her pithy words. Her tone was dry and her expression just as calm as usual, but I thought I saw amusement dancing in her eyes. Gathering my courage, I said, "I wanted to get it *myself.*"

"Why?"

I opened my mouth, then closed it again. No one had ever asked me *why* I did the things I did, at least not in a way that expected an answer. Laments and questions as to why I was determined to drive my various caretakers into early graves, yes. Honest inquiries, no.

"I—" I said, blinking. "I wanted to see if I could. I thought it would taste better if I could get it myself. I just," giving my head a little shake, I searched for words. "I just did."

"Hm, an adventurer," she said. "Well, little hellion," the epithet was familiar, but there was a fond note in the words that I wasn't sure what to do with, "what is it that you'd most like to do that you haven't been allowed to do?"

"Learn to sword fight," I said immediately, "and ride a horse like a man," I added in a hopeful addendum.

She frowned, and my heart leapt into my throat. Was she angry? She'd asked, but perhaps I shouldn't have told her. But her words surprised me. "You should certainly know how to ride a horse properly."

"I—I should?" I asked, hardly daring to hope.

"Indeed. What if the castle were attacked and you had to escape quickly?"

I stared at her, unable to answer.

"Sword fighting is trickier, but perhaps we can justify it as self-protection. After all, if someone were to try to kidnap you, you would want to be able to defend yourself, wouldn't you?"

"Yes!"

A half-smile tugged at her lips, though whether it was at my enthusiasm or some internal thought, I didn't know. Maybe she was merely amused by me. Rising from her seat, she said, "Here, help me get my overdress back on. If you are to learn sword fighting, there is something you must do first."

"What must I do?" I asked, eagerly finding her gold-embroidered robe and struggling to lift the heavy thing onto her shoulders. She slipped her hands into the sleeves, then turned and caught my upper arm, giving it a squeeze. I froze, staring at her and feeling my eyes go wide at the strange touch. She didn't speak, though. Instead she let go of me and expertly twisted her hair up into a far tighter, more regal configuration before asking me to help fasten the dress. Then, stepping out into the front room, she took me to the door and showed me the long hallway outside her chambers.

There was a servant scrubbing the floor at the end, a bucket and brush in her hand. Alcina looked up and down the hallway, nodded, and said, "When you can scrub the floor of this hallway from end to end in less than a day, then we will discuss your request once more."

A clatter drew our attention. The servant was staring up at us, her brush on the floor, her face pale. The queen did not smile.

"You," Alcina said to her. "Provide the princess with whatever she needs. This floor must be perfect. If I find so much as a speck of dirt, she will have to do it all again. And if I find that you or any other servant has helped her, I will be *very* displeased."

"Yes, your majesty. I mean, no, your majesty. I mean—" The poor woman, who didn't look much older than I was, threw herself on the floor. "It will be done, your majesty!"

"Good." Turning, she led the way back into her room and closed the door.

"You want me to scrub the floor?" I said, at least as stunned as the poor maid. "*Why?*"

Lifting an eyebrow at me, she said, "Do you want me to grant your request or not?"

"I do!"

"Accomplish this task and I will do so."

"But why—"

"I will tell you once you succeed. Oh, and," she added as though it was an afterthought, "you must stay current on all your studies as well."

"How am I supposed to do all my lessons *and* scrub that whole hallway in less than a day?"

She gave a one-shouldered shrug. "That is for you to figure out. What do your studies consist of?"

"The morning is history, economics and strategy," I said, and made a face as I added, "The afternoon is painting, music and embroidery."

"You do not enjoy the arts?" she said, the amusement back in her voice again, even if it didn't show on her face.

"I don't enjoy *those* arts." I would have loved to learn to cook. The idea of combining different flavors into an appealing dish fascinated me. I sometimes mixed the different items on my plate at dinner, attempting to come up with something new. At least, I'd done so until my nurse caught me and gave me a round scolding for 'playing with your food like a child'.

"Well, I will excuse you from your afternoon lessons for now," she said carelessly.

"*Really?*" I breathed.

"Yes, if you truly spend your time trying to accomplish the task I have assigned you without neglecting your morning studies."

"I will!" I said. "I will! Thank you, Alcina!" Acting on an impulse I'd never had before with anyone but my old nurse, I threw my arms around her. She stiffened, and for a moment I feared that I had ruined everything. Then she softened, one arm coming up to pat my back.

"You're welcome," she said, pulling away from me after a moment. I let her go, though a strange part of me longed to embrace her again, tighter, to bury my face in her hair and against her neck. She patted my cheek. "Silly," she chided me. "I am making you do a terrible and arduous task, and you are thanking me for it?"

"I am sure you have your reasons, stepmother," I replied.

A frown marred her lovely features. "Alcina," she corrected me.

"Alcina," I replied.

The maid, Esmerelda, brought me buckets and brushes and showed me how to clean the dirt from between the cracks in the stones as well as on the surface. She also demonstrated how sand and lye could be used to scrub off particularly stubborn stains. The entire time she wore an expression of pity that made me grit my teeth, but the more I told her that I was doing this task willingly, the more she seemed convinced that I was a good, obedient child and my stepmother was a monster.

I gave up trying to change her mind and set about learning my task. After two days my hands were chapped and blistered, my arms aching. Alcina called me in to see her that night, once again receiving me in her inner sanctuary, allowing me to see her as no one else, not even the servants, saw her: soft, loosened, undone.

Though I hid my hands behind my back, she demanded I show them to her. She took my chapped and raw fingers in her own smooth, cool ones, making tsking sounds as she inspected them. Letting them go, she turned and disappeared past one of the tapestries, through a door I hadn't even known existed. A whiff of strange smoke drifted out. I wondered if it was some foreign incense, spicy and not particularly pleasant. It tickled my nose and made me sneeze.

She returned with another billow of the odd smoke. I could hear a lock click and watched the tapestry fall back into place as she stepped into the bedroom bearing a small earthenware pot.

"Let me see your hands again," she said, and when I held them out, she proceeded to spread a soothing cream over them. "It will not speed the healing, but it will help with the pain."

Indeed, I could feel it working already, a soft numbness seeping through my poor fingers. "What is it?"

"Just a concoction I put together," she said. "You may take it with you and apply it again if it wears off during the night. Do not use it during the day. I'm afraid you must endure when you are awake, as the cream would make your hands too slippery and numb to do your lessons. But it should help you sleep, at least."

"Thank you, Alcina," I blurted out. "It's wonderful."

"Not at all," she scoffed, "It is merely a folk remedy. Oh, and you are not to scrub the floor for the next two days. Give your hands time to heal."

"But—!"

"No." Her expression took on the cold, implacable quality she normally showed to others outside her own space. "In the end it will take longer if you don't allow your body time to heal. You are building strength, but it does not happen overnight."

"Is that why you told me to scrub the floor? To build my strength?"

Her face closed off even more. "We will discuss it after you have completed the task I have assigned you."

"Yes, Alcina."

It took many weeks for me to build the necessary strength and stamina to scrub the entire hall from one end to the other. It wasn't easy work, but there was a satisfaction in it, in seeing the dirt come away. It wasn't a highly trafficked hallway, but enough servants passed along it tracking dirt of one kind or another or carrying trays of food that dripped, not to mention wax from candles, that keeping it clean was a challenge. The repetitive nature of the work gave me lots of time to think, and I often found myself considering my morning lessons, turning them over in my mind as I braced my arms and rubbed at a particularly stubborn stain. My tutors expressed surprise and pleasure that I seemed to be paying closer attention and retaining more of their teachings.

The rest of the time I thought about Alcina. Every few days, she would call me into her room in the evening and ask me how I was faring. At first I only told her how the hallway was coming along — *I made it almost to the halfway point today!* — but eventually I began slipping in other details, mostly thoughts on my lessons and sometimes things that had confused me.

She proved to be not only an insightful, clever, and well-read woman, but a good teacher. Difficult concepts became clear as water when she explained them, sometimes with stories, sometimes by calling for the servants to bring her a particular book from the royal library, which she would read aloud in a low, melodious voice.

Her voice was wonderful. It was low in pitch, a rich alto. It was almost enough to make me wish I'd continued with my music lessons after all. I imagined the duets we could have had, my soprano soaring above while her mellifluous notes flowed beneath.

Eventually I managed to complete the task she'd set for me. I negotiated with my tutors, requesting a day free from lessons if I worked extra hard during the rest of the week, and they, pleased by my progress, agreed. Taking my brushes and bucket, I began at one end of the hallway and, by the time the sun set, it was scrubbed entirely clean. I stood and stared at it for a long, satisfied moment. Soon enough someone would walk through, dirtying it again, but for this moment, it was spotless.

I'd taken to wearing an old, patched dress pressed on me by Esmerelda as I worked, and tying my hair back with a rag covering it. Now I looked down at myself and chuckled. No one coming into the castle from the outside would have thought that I was the royal princess. My hands were no longer soft, nor were they chapped and red. My skin had begun to develop a thicker consistency, with leathery callouses replacing the blisters.

Going to my stepmother's door, I dared to knock without being summoned first.

"Enter."

She stood in the front room, dressed in her gold brocade, her hands lightly clasped before her. When she saw me, her face broke into a smile. "Have you done it, then?"

At the time, I had no word for the emotion that rocked through me at the sight of her rare and precious display of joy or her pleasure at my accomplishment. I dropped into a low curtsey as I had not done since the beginning of our acquaintance, lowering my eyes to hide the way they stung. "Your majesty — Alcina — I have scrubbed the hallway as you asked. Please come and tell me if it is to your standards."

"Very well," she said, and I caught the note of humor beneath the words, which were usually so dignified. She stepped past me, taking a candle and inspecting the stone closely. I watched her, seeing the way she was so careful not to let a drop of wax drip onto the newly-cleaned floor, watching the way she genuinely checked for any speck of dirt, just as she'd promised.

When she had been back and forth over the long hallway twice over, she straightened and met my eyes. "It seems you have succeeded," she said, her voice cool, betraying no emotion whatsoever. There was a murmur from behind me, and I knew the servants were just around the corner, listening to us.

"Yes, your majesty," I said humbly, wanting all of them to know how much respect I held for Alcina.

"Come with me." She led me back to her room, closing the door behind her and setting down the candle. It wasn't until we were in the inner chamber that she smiled at me once more. "Well done, Snow White."

"Thank you, Alcina." Warmth spread out from my chest and down to my fingertips, even as my stomach did a funny little leap. It wasn't unpleasant, just strange and unfamiliar.

"Tomorrow afternoon you will begin sword fighting lessons. I have already discussed them with your teacher. He is a good man and a reliable one, with a great deal of experience fighting in war, not just in practice spars."

I reached out and caught one of her hands, startling her into silence. She blinked at me before looking away.

"Why did you tell me to scrub the floor?"

"Why do you think I did so?" she countered, regaining a little of her normal calm, though her cheeks seemed more flushed than usual.

"I was a spoiled, weak child, not allowed to run and play as other children," I said. "I didn't even have the strength to climb a tree without falling. If I'd tried to hold a sword in my soft hands, I probably would have dropped it. You wanted me to toughen my skin and strengthen my arms before you allowed me to try sword fighting for the first time."

Nodding, she ducked her head as though to hide the smile still playing on her lips. "There is more to it than that, though," she said. "What else?"

"You were testing my resolve," I said confidently. "If I could stay at this task, difficult and painful as it was at first, then I would not give up when it came to learning the sword."

"Very good," she said. There was warmth in her tone, and pride, and the heat in my own body seemed to increase. I

13

could feel my heart pounding and my face burning. "There is yet another reason. Can you guess it?"

I frowned. I gave it some thought, but no other ideas occurred to me. Embarrassed, I shook my head.

She lifted her head, her expression softening as she lay a hand on my shoulder. "If I merely wished for you to become stronger, there would have been other ways for you to do so. Why did I have you do such lowly work rather than something more suited to your station as a princess?"

"Because there isn't anything I could do that is suited to my station that would make me stronger?" I asked, knowing I was wrong even as I said it.

She shook her head. "You could have gotten much the same effect simply by starting your sword fighting lessons. In time you would have built strength and calluses. Why *this* way?"

"So as... not to waste the swordmaster's time?" I tried. When she shook her head again, I admitted, "I don't know."

"You are a princess," she said, her voice quiet but resonant. "Every person in the kingdom is your subject, from the lowliest chargirl who tends the fires and empties the chamber pots, to the most brilliant advisors and military leaders. All of them are people. It is but an accident of circumstance that you were born a princess and not a peasant."

"You wanted me to understand their point of view," I said slowly.

"I wanted you to have a taste of it," she said. "*You* had a choice. You could work as much or as little as you chose. You could stop when you were sick or hurting. You could work at a pace that wasn't too brutal. And your dinner and that of those you love wasn't dependent on you cleaning the entire hall in less than a day."

I stared, feeling my eyes widen and my mouth fall open. Her words weren't admonishing. Rather, they were sorrowful. Shame pricked at me. "*Alcina.*"

"You have done nothing wrong," she said, her voice gentle. "You were born a princess. You have been taught only to consider the larger picture. Sometimes difficult choices must be made: whether to let some people starve so that others might survive, perhaps, or whether to further burden those who are already weighed down with taxes in order to keep the kingdom strong and able to defend itself. I hope that you will consider the consequences of your choices on the common people, even if it makes the decisions harder for you in the end."

No tutor had ever spoken to me like this. "Alcina," I said, "who *are* you?"

"Don't you know?" she said to me, her eyes crinkling charmingly at the corners. "I'm a witch."

Chapter 2

From that day onward, my life changed. Alcina began to take over my tutoring, but she did not teach as my tutors had, with slate and books and dry words. Instead, she took me out of my school room and into the castle's storerooms. She showed me the supplies of grain, of vegetables, of dried meat and fish. She bade me sit at her own desk in her suite of rooms with a stack of account books, giving me instructions to find errors and add new entries. The neat columns of figures took on new and far more significant meaning when a mistake could mean that people wouldn't have enough to eat over the course of the winter.

She even began to share with me the messages she received, ones pleading for help, for mercy, for justice, for revenge. Then, too, she discussed with me the difficult decisions she faced while ruling the country in my father's absence, seeking my opinion and even my counsel. She had me search for answers in the castle's histories, so the stories that had once been dusty and dull came alive, made real by the quandaries faced by my own citizens here and now.

In short, she began training me to be a ruler, rather than the scholar my tutors had been trying to fashion me into.

As she took me through the records, I began to see a disturbing trend.

"Alcina," I said one day, lifting my head from the books filled with notes in her cramped yet legible hand, "I have a question."

She responded as she always did, turning to look at me

inquiringly, waiting for me to speak.

"Decades ago," I said slowly, trying to put my words to-gether in a way that made sense, "we were a rich kingdom, with stores of grain and a full treasury." She nodded, still waiting. "But in recent years, my father has waged endless wars on our neighbors. He has drained our coffers and used our stores, worn down our people and pressed our young men into battle." Alcina's expression remained solemn, and her eyes were sad. The tightness at the corner of her lips sug-gested anger.

"What is your question?" she asked.

It took me a moment to find what I wanted to say. "*Why?*" I burst out at last. "As far as I can see, these border disputes started over things that were petty and which should have been resolved easily."

There was something else in her gaze, now. Her eyes smiled at me, her cheeks lifting a little, pleased and proud. "Very good, Snow White," she said, and I felt my treacher-ously pale skin betray me, growing hot at her words. Sigh-ing, Alcina straightened and closed the book she was working on, a sign that she was serious and expected my full atten-tion. "Your father loved your mother very much," she began. "When she died, he grieved bitterly. And so, when the news came of an encroachment—or a supposed encroachment—on our land, instead of resolving it in a usual, reasonable way, with diplomacy or demand for reparations, he determined that he would take an army and fight. I think, perhaps, he hoped he would be killed in the skirmish. Instead, he found a new love: the thrill of battle. Our army, with the advantage of surprise and a determined leader, won the day. That victory sealed our fate."

I sensed that the 'our' she spoke of wasn't just the coun-try, but also the two of us. "He wanted to keep fighting," I said, horrified.

While my mornings were filled with lessons with Alcina, my afternoons were far more active, beginning with sword fighting lessons and ending with riding and caring for my horse, who I had romantically named 'Midnight'. Learning to fight with a sword had been thrilling and hard, leaving me aching and sweating and bruised. The swordmaster she had obtained for me was a veteran she called only "Gregory", an old man missing one eye who could nevertheless easily beat two younger men up and down the yard — and did so, by way of demonstration, when anyone dared question his prowess.

His stories of war had been nothing like the heroic tales I'd grown up learning. He spoke of men losing limbs, sickening and rotting after being wounded, dying in agony. Through him, I had come to hate the idea of battle. "It is sometimes a necessary evil," he said to me once. "But do not forget that it *is* evil."

"Yes, he wanted to keep fighting," Alcina echoed, drawing my attention back to the present. "I think he'd gone into it no longer caring if he lived or died, but during the fight he found the will to live again. He clung to that, sought it out, and turned our once peaceful country into a martial one. He revisited old disputes with our neighbors or manufactured new ones. What had once been minor skirmishes became major points of contention. Trade slowed and stopped, our young men were forced to become soldiers, leaving the burden of tending our fields on the shoulders of the too old and the too young. It came to consume him, until he could see nothing but his next battle, and forgot that the goal should have been peace. We grew less grain, mined more iron than gold, sold less to our neighbors, and gradually, our treasury was depleted."

"Can we not stop him?" I asked, my hands clenched into fists.

"He is the king."

I reeled back from the ring of hard finality in her tone. "But—"

"He is the king," she said again. "To speak against him is treason. Even for you."

I swallowed. "Alcina," I said, the question welling up from deep inside, "Why did you marry him?"

Her eyebrows went up, her eyes widening just a little. I'd surprised her. "He asked," she said simply. "And I hoped I could turn his thoughts to other things."

"But he wouldn't stay. Not even for you." Bitterness built thick and heavy in my throat.

"I was a passing fancy and a convenient substitute mother for his child." She shook her head, the distant look fading and a smile taking its place. "I don't regret it."

"No? Not even a little?"

"Not at all," she said. "If I hadn't married him, I would never have met you." She reached across to me and I wrapped her hand in both of mine.

"Do you know, it's been almost two years since we met?" Alcina said one night as I helped her remove the jewels and pins from her hair.

"That long?" My days had gone from an endless, dragging slog to being rich and full, falling into a happy pattern. Mornings I worked with Alcina and afternoons I practiced the sword. Alcina spent her afternoons holding court, listening to the endless line of supplicants and complaints, resolving disputes and doing all the things my father should have been doing. Afterward I would bathe, and the two of us would dine together. The evenings, to my delight, were our own.

Alcina relaxed with me as she did in front of no one else. As I carefully removed the last jeweled pin, making sure it didn't tangle, I was struck with an idea. "Shall I help you brush it tonight?" I asked lightly.

She was quiet for a moment, and I held my breath, wondering if I had overstepped. When she inclined her head in a nod, I felt a soaring thrill in my chest and a swoop deep in my belly.

As I unbound her golden tresses and began to run my fingers through them, gently combing them out, my own scalp prickled and a tingling ache rushed through my body. She was beautiful, but she was so much more than that. I hated my father for not seeing the truth of her: her cleverness, her goodness. But at the same time, I felt a selfish gratitude that I had so much of her all to myself.

"Thank you, Snow White," she said, her normally cool and distant voice turning warm and near. "That feels nice."

I slowed my fingers as much as I dared, slipping them along her scalp, massaging there and down the back of her neck. Her muscles were like iron bands under my fingers. With a groan, she allowed her head to fall forward.

"Of course, Alcina," I said, and was proud at how steady my voice was, "I'm happy to help."

"How go your sword fighting lessons?" she asked, the edges of her words so soft that they nearly bled into each other.

"Do you not receive regular reports from my teacher?" I teased.

She gave a nearly silent breath of laughter and said, "He tells me of your progress. I would know of your feelings. Do you still enjoy it? Do you wish to continue?"

"I love it," I admitted. "It is a challenge like none I have ever faced."

"You have gained a great deal of strength," she said, "and

you are healthier than you were. Your cheeks have roses in them these days."

"Not so 'snow white' anymore, then?"

"You will always be Snow White to me," she said, and my heart turned over within me. It was the name she had given me, the name she insisted all call me. I loved her for it, as I did for so many things.

We sat in silence for a time. I drew out my task as long as I dared, massaging her neck until it finally softened under my fingers. Eventually I had to move on to combing her hair, untangling it and loosely braiding it for the night. When I finally let my hands fall to my sides, she said, "Is there anything else you wish to learn or do?"

A confused desire rushed through me, to press close to her, to ask that she hold me, to feel her skin against mine. My face burned. "I would like to learn to cook," I blurted out.

"To cook?" She turned toward me, her eyebrows going up.

"It's interesting," I admitted. "Far more so than embroidery or music. The process of taking raw ingredients and transforming them into a finished meal... it's like magic."

She gave a gurgle of laughter and shook her head. "It's nothing like magic," she said, "not like *true* magic, though it is very much like what most would call magic. As always, you manage to be both silly and wise," she said fondly. "Very well. You shall learn about cooking. But as with sword fighting, you must earn it."

I straightened my back and lifted my chin. "What must I do?"

A few months later I was working in the kitchen, scrubbing pots and pans, when the voice of one of the kitchen maids came to my ears.

"Poor girl," she said. "Why does her stepmother hate her so? She is gentle and dutiful, cheerfully doing all that she's asked."

"I heard her stepmother is jealous of her beauty," came the whispered response. "And that's not all. I've even heard that the queen is a witch. She enthralled the king and plans to remove his daughter so that no one can contest her right to the throne."

I scowled and scrubbed harder. It wasn't the first time I'd heard such rumors, but they'd never been so blatant. I'd tried to correct them at first — explaining that I was doing this of my own free will, that my stepmother had her reasons — but it only ever caused people to look at me with more pity. Such a good, obedient, child, they said! When only a year ago I had run wild, causing these same servants no end of trouble. How short people's memories were.

"The queen even had her work as a *chambermaid* for a month," muttered one of the kitchen girls in obvious horror.

My lips quirked as I rinsed the pot and set it aside, reaching for another. It hadn't been the most pleasant of my duties, but it had been educational. "If you're going to be making food," Alcina had said to me, "You should know where it comes from, but also where it ends up." By comparison, kitchen duty was positively pleasant.

"If you have time to gossip," came the deep voice of the cook, "then you have time to work." I felt some of the tension ease from my shoulders. She was a formidable woman, with sharp eyes and no tolerance for nonsense. She'd accepted my addition to her domain without a flicker of either pity or favoritism, much to my relief.

"Are you done with that?" she said to me as the other girls scattered like a flock of birds startled by a hawk. "Good. We need to whip some cream for the dessert tonight."

I swallowed a groan and dried my hands. Despite the strength I'd built while studying the sword, whipping cream and beating eggs left my arms sore and aching afterward. I reminded myself that I'd asked for this, and went to get the cream out of the cellar.

I drooped and yawned over my studies. Alcina watched me with calm eyes, a hint of worry in her expression. "Perhaps we should reduce your sword fighting practice time after all."

"No!" I said, sitting up. We'd already discussed this more than once. In the year and a half since Alcina had come to the castle, my days had gone from being empty to being filled, and then from being filled to being overstuffed. Alcina would not budge on the importance of my studies in the morning, while I refused to give up any of my precious sword fighting and horseback practice in the afternoon. That left little time for the new duties she'd assigned me: first, the month with the chamber pots before she'd let me anywhere near the kitchen, then another month doing nothing but scrubbing dishes and pots and pans, learning to polish the silver until it shone. Only after that had I been allowed to help cook, beginning with the simplest of recipes. In the succeeding months I had gradually worked my way up from learning to crack an egg and boil water to being able to bake a cake, though not without some mishaps.

When I'd been handling the chamber pots I'd had to start rising earlier, and once I'd graduated to kitchen duty I stayed on the same schedule, spending the early hours and lunchtime preparing food that would be consumed shortly after. I was always busy. It was satisfying but admittedly exhausting.

"When you take on too much, your memory suffers," Alcina said, the worry in her eyes tempered by a sudden light of mischief. "Didn't you tell me you'd forgotten to add sugar to the cake you were baking last week?"

I groaned. "That was one time!" I said. "And at least I learned something from it."

"That a cake without sugar is not as sweet?" she teased.

"The cake was denser and it didn't turn brown," I said earnestly. "Not to mention how dry it was when I tried it."

She shook her head, a bemused smile on her lips. "Two years ago I never would have dreamed that the notorious princess of the realm would be so fascinated by the art of cooking."

My lips pressed into a pout. "Learning how the addition or subtraction of a particular ingredient changes the outcome is fascinating," I said, a touch sullenly.

"I'm glad you're enjoying it," Alcina said. "I just worry that you are exhausting yourself."

"I'm fine," I said. "A real cook works more hours than I do in a day. I'm not *frail*."

"Very well," she sighed, the unhappy frown still marring her lovely brow. I reached across and smoothed my fingers over it, which brought a wry smile to her lips. "You charm even me," she said.

A confused rush of pleasure and longing welled in me at her words. I brushed it aside, as I'd become good at doing. "I will be alright," I insisted. "Soon I will be able to cook a meal for you!"

"I look forward to it," she said with perfect sincerity. She turned the page, then hesitated, her hand on the book. Straightening, she closed the volume and said, "Actually, this is relevant to some upcoming plans I wish to discuss."

I set aside my own book and gave her my full attention.

"How old are you now?" she asked.

"Eighteen," I said, resisting the urge to add "nearly nineteen" like a child.

"Yes, it is a good time for this. I have arranged a tour of the kingdom. We will be visiting farmers, butchers, and many others so that you may learn more about where the food you are preparing comes from."

"I'll be leaving the castle?" I said, excitement swelling within my chest like a soufflé in an oven, light and fragile.

"We'll be leaving the castle," she said. "We won't be going far. It will mostly be a series of day trips over the course of a month, leaving early and returning by nightfall."

"What about my lessons?" I asked. "What about my practice?"

"Both will be suspended."

"But I can't take a month off of practice!" The excitement faltered, the soufflé trembling.

She said, with a sigh, "You will have an hour after we return each day during which you may drill if you insist on doing so. But consult with your swordmaster whether it's necessary or not. He will know better than you. The rest may be a good thing."

"Yes, Alcina," I said. The servants would no doubt comment on how dutiful I was if they heard me. It brought to mind the gossip I'd overheard on more than one occasion. "Alcina," I said slowly, "I have a question."

She met my eyes, placid and expectant.

"Why do you allow people to think that you're cruel? Especially to me?" As I spoke the words, my thoughts and memories crystalized. "You rule fairly, but speak no kind or gentle words when you do so. You let people believe that you are a hard woman with a cold heart. They think you forced me into servitude. They call you a witch."

"I am a witch," she said, as calm as ever. She had told me such before, but lightly and laughingly, as though it was a joke. This time she spoke as though it was a straightforward truth. A chill ran down the back of my neck. The punishment for witchcraft could be severe. "And as for the rest," she began to undo her hair, perhaps just to have something to do with her hands. I moved to help her, though my shoulders were aching. "Thank you," she murmured, "as for the rest, once I saw that your father's attraction to me was fleeting and self-serving, I knew that it would not last. Men tend to kill women they tire of, especially when they are men with power."

The chill spread to my stomach and chest. "He won't kill you!"

"Perhaps not," she said. "But there is a good chance that he will wish to marry again, and I will be in the way. Once you are fully grown, I will have served my purpose, and will merely be an impediment."

"An *impediment*," I snarled. As though my lovely, kind Alcina were simply something to be used when convenient and discarded when she was no longer.

"It is not uncommon," she said, as matter-of-fact as though she was speaking of the weather. I pulled a tangle a little too hard. When she winced, I dropped the comb as though I'd burned her.

"I'm sorry," I said, but she turned and smiled at me.

"It's nothing," she said. "I am far more vicious when I comb it myself."

"I wish you wouldn't be," I said, knowing it was useless even as the words left my mouth. Alcina was always hardest on herself. This woman who deserved warmth more than anyone else I knew, who accepted every gentle touch from me like a dry plant drinking up water, be it when I combed her hair or helped her dress or pressed up next to her when she was showing me something in a book. I had not yet dared suggest we bathe together, but I had thought about it a great deal.

"Snow White," she said softly, "I have long accepted what my fate will be. I do not wish for death, nor will I seek it out. When the king tires of me, if I can, I will leave and return to my old life. But it is likely that he will not allow me to do so."

"I will not let him kill you," I vowed.

"You will not have a choice. They will say that I enthralled you as they think I enthralled him."

"But why?" I cried. "You could have shown your kindness and gentleness to the people, and they would have loved you!" *They would have loved you as I do,* I did not say.

"Because it wouldn't have made a difference in the end." She bent to pick up the dropped comb, fiddling with it as she spoke. "I am strange and different: my hair light where most in this land are dark; I am an unknown woman who once lived alone in the forest. At least this way, my death will have some use."

"What? What *use?*"

"Before I came, you were the wild princess, a scamp at best and a troublemaker at worst. A poor, motherless girl who'd been spoiled and a wild creature that would be better suited to being turned loose in the woods than ruling the country. Or so people said." I reached for the comb, but she stayed my hand with hers, wrapping it around my fingers. "Now, you are a good, obedient, diligent young woman whose cruel stepmother abuses her terribly. In turning them against me, I have made them love you."

"I don't want their love if it costs your life!" I gripped her hand and swallowed back tears.

"If my life is forfeit either way, better that my death have value and meaning."

"There is no value or meaning in death! What meaning can my life have if you are gone?" I flung away from her, tears spilling out as they had not in years. I wasn't grieving, I was *furious.*

She was silent. Eventually she spoke, regret tinging her voice. "Perhaps I should have treated you coldly," she said. "I had planned on doing so. But when I met you... I found I could not."

My heart twisted at that admission. Imagining Alcina treating me with the same cold distance she showed everyone else made me want to curl into myself. Relief and gratitude that she had not done so nearly had me throwing myself at her feet. "Why couldn't you?" I said, unable to keep my voice from wavering.

"I don't know," she said. "Perhaps it was simply that I recognized in you a reflection of myself."

"A reflection?"

"You were alone. I was as well."

The rage leapt high again. My chest burned with it, angry sobs choking me. How dare my father make her feel this way? How dare he let her place so little value in herself? I stomped my foot like a child and cried, "C-couldn't we make them hate my father instead? H–He's the one draining our country dry with his incessant wars."

"No we could not," she said, sounding cross for the first time in memory. "He is the king. It doesn't matter if the people love him or hate him. He will do as he pleases either way."

"But—"

"And as for meaning, the greatest meaning will be for you to marry the son of our strongest enemy and bring peace to both countries."

I couldn't speak or move for several long seconds. I flinched as the full import of her words sank in. "*What?*"

"You are a princess," she said implacably. "You have read the histories with me."

"This is my greatest value? To sell myself for the hope of peace as," my body went tight with understanding, "as *you* did?"

"It is your duty," she said simply, and I turned and fled to my own room, where I could throw myself onto my bed and weep in fury without interruption.

When I went to my normal lessons the following morning, Alcina greeted me with a subdued "Good morning." She was stiff and pale, and my rage, which I had stoked and burned with for half the night, died to ashes, leaving me cold and tired.

"I'm sorry," I said, seating myself next to her. She had long since taken over my former school room, removing the heavy velvet curtains to let in more light and setting up a long table we could work at together, side by side.

"What for?" she said. I subtly leaned into her and felt her stiffen further, then relax, pressing back slightly, her shoulder to mine.

"I know you're doing what you think best," I said slowly, feeling out the words. "But I cannot so cavalierly accept the idea of your death. How would you feel if our positions were reversed?"

I turned to watch her expression as I spoke. Her eyes widened, her brows drawing into a frown. When she spoke, it was with a heavy certainty.

"I—I would want to save you," she admitted.

"Yet you ask me to marry someone who could tire of me and discard me?"

"To bring peace back to the land? Perhaps," she said. "But you misunderstand. I had hoped that you might find joy, perhaps even love. The prince is said to be both handsome and kind—"

29

"And I am said to be gracious and obedient," I scoffed. "We both know the worth of such rumors."

She acknowledged my point with a bitter little twist of her lips. "True. But I did not intend for you to marry him without knowing him first. I have arranged," her hands gave a nervous little flutter in her lap, "that is, he is coming here."

"What?" I exclaimed. "When?"

"After our tour of the kingdom. He will be visiting under a flag of truce. His mother and I have had some correspondence."

A flare of jealousy made me wrinkle my nose. "You've been exchanging letters with her?"

"Only regarding official matters," she replied, her mouth lifting at one corner for the first time that morning. "Such as the potential marriage of our children."

"I'm not your child," I snapped.

"Such as the potential marriage of the eligible prince and princess of our respective kingdoms," she corrected herself smoothly.

I pressed my lips together against the words that wanted to spill out: I had no interest in this prince or any other. I failed to see why I should sell my life to solve a problem caused by my father. I wanted more than anything to stay by Alcina's side.

"Please," she said, "at least meet with him. Give him a chance." She had never begged me for anything. I swallowed.

"Very well."

Chapter 3

The month-long tour of the kingdom went by faster than I could have imagined, a whirlwind of meeting countless new people.

"This is no place for a woman," snorted a butcher, but when he saw that I didn't flinch from slicing open a carcass and draining it of blood, he changed his tune, admitting, "You're stronger than I expected."

"We are using wood faster than we can replenish it," the head of the carpenter's guild told me, and I watched his expression turn to one of respect when Alcina and I listened to him, asking for his ideas on how to grow more wood more quickly while lessening our usage of it.

"There aren't enough people to help gather crops," a farmer with a weathered face explained. "My sons were both taken into the army." There was little I could say to that, but I recruited the teenaged daughters of the next-nearest farm to help the older man.

Before I knew it, I was home again. I'd spoken with butchers and dairy maids as Alcina had promised, but also merchants and tradesman from all walks of life. I learned more in those few days about the people of my kingdom than my tutors had ever tried to teach me in the years I'd been under their care.

Returning to my daily pattern felt strange. And no sooner had I begun to settle into the routine again than Alcina said one evening, "Prince Karl will arrive in two days."

My lips twisted into a displeased moue.

"You promised you would give him a chance," Alcina said reproachfully.

"I did," I sighed.

The man who greeted me with polished words of gratitude for our hospitality and a perfectly-executed bow was handsome enough, I supposed, though younger than I'd expected. He was fair, but his hair was a muddier gold than the brilliant honey-shade of Alcina's. His eyes had hints of gray, unlike the striking, pure blue of hers.

If I had not known and loved Alcina, if I had remained a lonely princess in a castle filled with people who could not be my equals and who did not understand me, perhaps I would have reached out to the young prince and held on with both hands. He would have been the first person I'd ever met who was both close to my own age and someone over whom I did not hold the power of life and death.

But as he was Alcina's chosen partner for me, I was quite prepared to hate him. I kept my face impassive and cold, trying to imitate Alcina and her imperturbable facade.

He matched me, responding with practiced politeness but without warmth.

We might have gone on like that for his entire visit, a carefully orchestrated dance with pre-planned movements, had not the careless words of his retainer given me a glimpse beneath the prince's carefully cultivated exterior.

We held a welcome banquet for him and his retinue, of course. (Alcina forbade me from helping prepare it, much to my disgust.) One of the prince's followers, an older man, drank glass after glass of wine, his sallow complexion slowly becoming flushed. During the fourth course, he began mumbling, and the more he drank, the louder he grew. By the time the last course was being set out on the table, the man burst out with a garbled complaint, but the words "warmongering king" rang through the room with the force of a bell.

"You forget your place," snapped Prince Karl. He turned to me and said graciously, "I do apologize. He is unused to long journeys, and his tolerance is nearly as low as mine. I remember one time," he began, launching into a self-deprecating story that had the entire table in an uproar of laughter by the end, regardless of where they were from.

A grudging respect crept up on me as I watched the performance. But it was after the attention shifted away from him that I saw it: the way his tense shoulders slumped slightly with relief, and the exasperation in his eyes as he looked at his retainer the way one might look at an unruly younger brother. I caught his eye and he startled, then gave me a private, rueful smile.

It was the first time I'd met anyone other than Alcina who understood the burden we carried. I found I could not hate him after that.

He seemed to feel the same, though I did try to discourage it. The afternoon of the second day he was there, I challenged him to a spar.

"A spar?" he asked in clear disbelief. "With swords?"

"No, with bread loaves," I replied acerbically. "Of course with swords, what else?"

Rather than disgusted, he seemed bemused by the idea. When I showed up in the practice yard in my carefully-tailored training clothes, designed to allow me freedom of movement, his eyebrows went up, but I did not read condemnation in his gaze. And when we began to fight, after a few quick feints, he did not hold back.

I fought him to a draw, my sword at his throat and his

sword poised to run me through. He laughed then, the sound clear and open in the sun-drenched air.

"Your highness," he said, stepping back and making a respectful bow, "I never thought to find such a skilled opponent in a potential marriage partner."

The thrill of the fight soured. I scowled, realizing that I had no one to blame but myself. Much as Alcina had discovered with me, I found I could not follow through on my plans to remain cold and distant...not in the face of his warmth. He was a kindred spirit. Despite everything, I liked him.

But I did not wish to marry him.

Perhaps my expression gave me away, when my smile abruptly turned to dismay.

We were both trained in the art of diplomacy. He went on the attack with a blunter question than he'd asked in the entire time he'd been there. "Is the idea of marrying me so displeasing?" he asked, his voice quiet.

"No, it's just that I have no wish to be married to anyone." I would be happiest living out my days at Alcina's side, I thought.

He nodded, his brows drawing together into a thoughtful frown. "I wish for nothing more than peace between our peoples," he said. "I have vowed to do whatever is necessary to bring about that end."

"Even marry a wild princess like me?" I asked with a half-smile.

"I do not think it would be a burden, to marry you," he said slowly, but not enthusiastically. "You are clever and skilled and determined, and you care for your people. You would not be a useless, languishing flower like some princesses I have met. Some princes, too," he added with a spark of humor.

"You don't wish to be married, either," I said, struck by sudden inspiration. "At least, not to me."

His eyes flickered, the smile dying out of them. I wondered to whom he had given his heart. "Does it matter what we want?" he said. "We have a duty."

Oh, how I hated that word. I hated that he sounded like Alcina, and that he was right. "We do," I said. "But what if we could find a way to bring about peace that didn't involve marrying each other?"

"Is there such a way?" he asked. "Even now your father wages his endless war upon us. No matter what we have tried or conceded, he has demanded more, becoming increasingly unreasonable. There seems to be no satisfying him."

Familiar rage rose in me. "I know," I said, ashamed. My father's selfishness had brought about so much unnecessary suffering.

"And even if you find a way to appease him or cure him of his bloodlust," Prince Karl said frankly, "these years of war have left a rift between our peoples. Many have died to the swords of the other side. Many have lost sons, brothers, husbands, fathers to 'the enemy'. It may not be possible to even begin to close this rift except through something as symbolic as binding our families in marriage."

I looked away, my hand tightening on my sword hilt. "I understand," I said. "I will consider your proposal."

"Thank you," he said. He glanced at my sword, then up at me, then around at the mostly-empty yard. "Want to go another round?"

I grinned.

Prince Karl left without pressing me for an answer. We had no more time to discuss things privately after that stolen afternoon (I learned later that it had been Alcina's doing to make sure we were left nominally alone and uninterrupted in the practice yard, though of course a small contingent of trusted guards from both sides had been watching over us from a distance the entire time.)

Our conversation occupied my thoughts for several days, until my life was disrupted once again when we received word that my father was returning home.

A part of me balked at the idea of sharing Alcina with him, and I told it very sternly that she would be happier with her husband at home, paying attention to her as he should be, rather than off waging wasteful war. If he spent more time with her, he would surely come to see how wonderful she was.

The thought didn't help, so I threw myself into my various duties even harder, training and working and learning all I could. At night I would sit exhausted on the floor next to Alcina's chair, my head in her lap, and she would read to me.

When my father came home at last, it was nothing like I'd thought it would be.

He arrived late, tired and dirty and demanding food and a bath. When the servants rushed to provide them, I, awakened by the commotion, nearly ran into him in the hallway. I was still in my nightgown, my hair loose, and he took one look at me and paled as though he'd seen a ghost.

"Father?" I asked, rubbing my eyes.

"Ah," he said, shaking his head. "It's nothing. Nothing at all. What are you doing here?"

"You made such a ruckus," I said, tired enough not to bridle my tongue, "how could I sleep through it?"

There was a flicker of something across his face—not anger, as I'd half-expected, but wide-eyed wonder. "My apologies," he said, and it was my turn to be surprised. An apology was the last thing I'd expected from my harsh-tongued father.

"It's all right," came Alcina's voice. She stepped into the hall, fully dressed, her hair in a hasty twist. "How could we object to having you back again, no matter when you arrive?" she said to him with a warm smile.

He looked between us, his face folded into what looked like a perplexed frown.

With a light step, she moved to his side and laid a gentle hand on his arm. "Come, Richard. A bath has been drawn for you. You must be eager to wash away the dust of the road." He glanced down to where she touched his forearm and his frown deepened, but he allowed himself to be led away. He cast one last lingering look at me over his shoulder as he left.

I rose early the next morning, the habit having long been ingrained by now. My father was asleep, I was told, and so I went to my 'schoolroom' to await Alcina.

It should not have been a surprise that she didn't join me there.

I spent the morning studying and, after much consideration, told Gregory that I would not be attending training that day or for the foreseeable future. I did not know how my father would react if he learned of it, and I didn't want to do anything that might jeopardize it. What he didn't know about he couldn't forbid.

After that first day I found myself wishing that he would leave again, the sooner the better. Sternly, I took myself to task. Alcina's happiness, and the happiness and well-being of my kingdom was more important than such petty jealousies, or so I told myself.

In fact, I decided, I should speak to my father and convince him to cease waging war upon our neighbors. I envisioned myself pleading with him and bringing him to see the harm he was inflicting upon his kingdom and his people quite unnecessarily. Surely I could get him to see reason, if only I could explain it to him.

Yet once I decided to undertake this noble task, the opportunity to speak to him never seemed to come.

The day after he arrived, I was informed by a servant that he and the queen would dine privately. I asked the servant to convey a message that I wished to speak to him, then repaired to my room, alone. Though I stayed up reading until I could no longer keep my eyes open, he never summoned me.

Whenever I sought him out, he always seemed to be somewhere else. When I did manage to find him, he was invariably busy with one thing or another, surrounded by people. He would catch sight of me and frown that same puzzled frown before his attention was drawn by something else, or Alcina swept him away, his name always on her lips.

The days that followed were much the same. I kept trying to see my father and kept finding myself thwarted. It was good that he was spending so much time with Alcina, I told myself, trying to ignore the hollow pit in my core. Perhaps he would remain home from now on.

But would it really be worth it, an irrepressible and selfish part of me asked, if it meant that I never got to spend time with Alcina again?

Alcina finally showed up at my room on the third day after his arrival. She brought new dresses for me, insisting that I wear them. I could not understand why. They seemed rather childish even to my inexperienced eyes, cut to minimize my already small bust and falling straight past such curves as my sword training had left me. Their colors all sat oddly against my pale skin, soft pinks and peaches that made me disappear, and yellows and light greens that made me look pallid and ill. I'd always favored bold colors, on the rare occasions I'd thought about such things at all, and Alcina had once told me that dark colors looked best with my complexion. It occurred to me, as I frowned down at one dress in a particularly objectionable shade of puce, that she wished for me to wear clothes that were unflattering. I could not fathom why. Was it simply part of her campaign to be taken as a cruel and abusive stepmother? Yet I was convinced that there was some other reasoning behind it.

"Why do you wish me to wear these?" I asked her, but she only shook her head, her eyes strained and the corners of her lips drawn tight.

"Please," she said, "wear them."

I was helpless to refuse her. "Very well, since you ask it," I said, and watched her shoulders loosen with obvious relief.

"Thank you," she said, and turned to leave.

"I wish to speak to my father," I called after her. She stopped and turned, the tension rushing back into her frame.

"Why?"

"I will convince him to stop waging war on our neighbors," I said.

"And what makes you think he will listen to you?" Alcina's voice was hard.

"I'm his daughter," I replied, reaching for the confidence I'd felt only a moment ago. "He'll listen to what I have to say."

"Will he?" There was an odd note in her voice now, a bitter, mocking tone I'd never heard her use in private, and only rarely in public. "You are a child. What would you know of such things?"

"I just want the chance to speak with him!"

"It's best if you stay out of his way."

I stared at her. Her words were cold and her face might as well have been carved from stone. She met my eyes without a trace of her usual warmth. It made my chest feel tight. I searched for words. "Why?" I said at last.

"You will not be able to convince him. Do you think others haven't tried?"

"But I'm his daughter!" I repeated. My voice sounded thin and uncertain in my ears.

"Which is exactly why he won't listen to you. No man wishes to be lectured by his own child, especially his daughter. You must stay away from him."

In all the time I'd spent with Alcina, she'd never been so implacable. So *unreasonable*. Anger and hurt swirled in my stomach. I lifted my chin and felt my lips tightening. "And if I say I will not?"

Her eyes widened at my display of defiance. "Then I will lock you in your room."

Angry tears sprang to my eyes. When I had misbehaved as a child, my father had once ordered me locked in my room for a week. But Alcina had never even threatened to do such a thing. Always, she had listened to what I had to say, an island of calm reason against my storm of emotions. I didn't understand what could have changed.

A peremptory knock on my door disrupted our argument. I seethed as I went to answer it, then pulled up short when I saw who was standing in the doorway. "Father?"

"Yes," he said. His gaze rested on my face, strangely intense. "I wished to speak with you."

Alcina stepped forward. "Your majesty," she began, but I interrupted her.

"What is it, father?"

He looked between us, his eyes narrowing. "I have been hearing disturbing rumors about your treatment of my daughter," he said to Alcina, his tone biting. "I came to ask her if they were true, and here I find you threatening to lock her in her room." I stared, stunned by his hypocrisy. Realization crept over me, Alcina's words echoing in my ears: *I will have served my purpose, and will merely be an impediment.*

The bottom dropped out of my stomach. "Father, no," I said quickly. "Alcina has been good to me."

His gaze returned to me, and softened. "You are a good girl," he said, "I will not allow her to crush your spirit."

"She's — she's not, I promise! Father, I — "

He shook his head and shot an unfriendly look at Alcina that sent a spike of terror through my heart. "You need not fear her any longer," he said to me.

"I *don't!* Please, father, listen to me!" I darted forward and caught his hand in both of mine. "Alcina is wonderful! You would see that if only you would stay home and not keep fighting these stupid, pointless wars!"

He stiffened. "Stupid? *Pointless?*" he said, his voice low and angry.

"They are!" I cried, too overwhelmed to temper my response. "They're draining our country dry!"

"So you would instead allow our enemies to run roughshod over us? Give up our kingdom into their hands without a fight?" he said harshly.

"Of course not!" I shouted, my head so hot with rage that I thought my skin would burn off in a moment. "But war is not the only possible solution! You must realize that!"

His head rocked back as though he'd been slapped, and he sucked in a sharp breath. "You're so like her," he whispered.

It was the last thing I expected him to say. "Like — what?" I said, faltering. "Like who?"

"Margareta," he whispered. I recoiled, but he caught my hand again, now gripping it in his. "You look just like her. You sound like her." His eyes pleaded.

My name was on his lips, but he wasn't addressing me. I yanked away from him, nausea rising in my throat.

I had been named for my mother.

"Snow White is her own person," my stepmother snapped.

My father turned to her, a strange smile on his lips. "You

have enthralled her," he said, "and sought to turn her against me."

"She hasn't!" I cried. "Father, you—"

"Quiet."

The single word carried the command of a king. I choked on my words, helpless horror spilling through me.

Another knock interrupted us. The king answered it, glaring at the servant. "Well?"

"Y-your majesty," he stammered. "A messenger has arrived. There has been another incursion—"

Giving an irritated hiss, my father looked from me to Alcina, then turned away. "I'll deal with both of you when I return," he tossed at us as he left. Both of us stood where we were as he slammed the door behind him and the sound of his voice barking out orders disappeared down the hallway. When it was silent again, I stumbled over to the bed and let my knees give way at last.

"What have I done?" I said, pressing my palms to my eyes. There was a soft touch on my shoulder, and then I was drawn into gentle arms. "Alcina," I whimpered.

"It's all right," she said. "He would not have listened to reason no matter what you said. It was not you he was seeing."

"But—" I sobbed.

"Hush," she said. "Now is not the time to give in to tears. We must plan."

"P-plan?" I struggled to master myself, and allowed myself the luxury of winding my arms around her soft body and clutching her close for a long moment before letting go and scrubbing my face.

"You must leave the castle."

"What? Why?" I felt a handkerchief pressed into my hand and lifted it to my face. "Why would *I* have to leave? You're the one he—"

"Come with me." My heart leapt. Of course! We would

leave the castle together. We would flee and start a new life. "Come to my room," she said, dashing my hopes. "I have something to show you."

Used to obeying her, I dried my tears and followed her out. She glanced up and down the hallway before leading me back to her own chambers. Once there, she locked the door and took me into her bedroom, to the tapestry I'd once seen her disappear behind.

She led me through the door hidden there into a short, dark hallway, and then to another door, this one without any apparent keyhole or handle. Lifting a hand, she placed it on the wood. A sigil flared to life beneath her fingers, the light spilling into the dark, narrow space, and the door swung inward.

My breath caught in my throat. "True magic," I murmured.

She nodded distractedly before leading me inside. "This space was the only thing I requested of your father when I married him. A private space of my own, in which to pursue my studies. One the servants did not know about and would not dare to enter if they did." Her voice echoed slightly off the stone walls.

The chamber wasn't large, but it was filled with all manner of things, some recognizable, most strange. A single lantern flickered near the entrance. More of the room became visible as Alcina took a taper and began to light other lanterns, one in each corner. The wall on the right was hung with a huge collection of what looked like dried spices in small cheesecloth bags, each tied with a different color ribbon. Various scents swirled around the room, some familiar to me from the time I'd spent in the kitchens: cinnamon, cloves, garlic.

On the left was a long wooden table strewn with all manner of items. What appeared to be small piles of gems and bits of precious metals sparkled and shone, while further down, clear vials of various mysterious substances sat lined up: red as blood, black as night, white as snow. A stack of books sat toward the end—a couple of thick tomes, but mostly thin, loosely-bound volumes, barely books at all.

The most prominent feature of the room glinted on the wall opposite the doorway, and it was to this that Alcina went directly after lighting the lanterns, not even looking at the rest of the room. A large mirror in an ornate gold frame hung there, a giant oval almost as tall as a person.

"What is it?" I asked.

I half expected her to tease me by saying, 'It's a mirror,' but she answered me seriously. "A spirit of beauty lives within its depths," she said. "For years I have asked it to show me who your father thinks is the most beautiful woman in the land. When his attention finally began to stray, I wanted to have warning. But it always showed myself...until two days ago."

"The day after he arrived home," I breathed. The nausea returned. "Who did it show?" I asked, fearing the answer.

"Spirit," she said, addressing the mirror in a sing-song cadence:

> Show to me the king's truth,
> The one that he
> Finds most beautiful in all the land.

The surface of the mirror swirled as though filled with smoke, then cleared again, and I saw my own pale face reflected back at me. Before I could ask if it was working, it fogged over and cleared again, showing my father snapping out orders to a man I recognized as his most trusted advisor. I could tell the two of them were alone in his chambers. "—and when I return," he said, his voice faint but audible, "we shall be married."

"Married? But—" his advisor stammered, "—you cannot marry your own daughter, your majesty."

He laughed strangely. "She's not my daughter," he said.

"She is the spirit of my wife, reborn. I can see it in her eyes, she has the same passion, the same fire. Ah, Margareta."

My stomach twisted violently and I had to swallow down bile. Until that moment, I had never minded being named after my mother.

"What of your current wife?" said his poor advisor. "She has been a good queen in your absence and—"

"She is a witch," said my father coldly. The advisor went silent. "She has enthralled many of you, it seems, though she has made little effort to hide what she is. Perhaps her death will snap the bonds she has used to ensnare Margareta and the rest of you."

"Y-your majesty," his advisor whispered, "surely—"

"Margareta is the most beautiful woman in the land," my father said, serene. "Once she is freed of her stepmother's toils, she will love me again."

"Yes, your majesty."

"This latest incursion is more important than any of that," my father said, waving a hand dismissively as though my future and Alcina's life weighed nothing in the balance. "Witch or no, the queen will continue to handle the court in my stead until I can return."

The mirror went dark.

"He's mad," I whispered. "He's—how can he—"

Alcina's hands gripped my shoulders, firm and grounding. "After he rides out, you must leave the castle," she said. "It must be tonight. I have a place you can go."

"Only if you come with me," I said.

"I cannot," she said. I shuddered and opened my mouth to protest, but she continued, "I must stay and rule in his place. He will not let it be publicly known that I am a witch yet, not until he returns. He is strong-willed and his mind is more and more unbalanced, but I have his True name. It gives me a little power to sway him even now. After he leaves tonight I will pretend that you are ill and staying in your room. With the help of my magic, I can maintain the illusion for a time. For months if necessary. The longer we can do so, the better."

"When he returns," I said bleakly, "he'll kill you."

"I will escape and come to you," she said. I threw myself forward, into her arms.

"Promise?" I begged.

"Yes," she said, and I tried not to hear the echo of my own hopelessness in her voice: *could* she escape, with the king no doubt pursuing her at every turn? "I promise." Too soon, she released me and stepped back. Raising a hand, she slipped it behind her neck. After a moment she drew a necklace from beneath her clothes, holding it carefully so that it didn't slip off its chain. I caught a flash of the pendant in the moonlight before she stepped forward and fastened it around my neck, the metal still warm from her skin. "Do not open it and do not take it off," she said. I bowed my head in acknowledgement and startled when I felt warm lips against my forehead in a kiss that both lingered oddly and yet felt far too short.

"I promise," I whispered in turn.

Chapter 4

We left in the dead of night. My only companion was Gregory, the man who'd taught me to use a sword. The work I'd done learning to ride a horse 'properly', as Alcina had said, turned out to be mostly wasted. I could not take my own mount lest my absence be discovered too soon. Instead I was obliged to ride pillion on Gregory's sturdy warhorse, wrapping my arms around his broad back and holding on. The smell was overwhelming, sweat and leather and horse. More than anything I wished that it was Alcina sharing the horse with me, my arms around her slender waist, my face pressed to her hair and the back of her neck. Or perhaps the other way, me guiding the horse, her behind me, flush against my body, holding on for dear life.

We rode half the night, quickly leaving the capital and making our way into the woods. As we left the city and villages behind our path grew dense and dark, forcing us to slow our pace. "Where are we going?" I dared to ask him once the last straggling lights of humanity had disappeared.

"Where her majesty told me to take you," he grunted.

I considered asking him where that might be, but I already knew he wouldn't tell me. Instead I said, "You are loyal to her." I knew she would not have sent me with anyone she didn't trust completely.

"Yes."

"Why?" I spoke quietly, but even so it sounded loud. We'd muffled the metal parts of the tack with cloths and tied rags around his horse's metal-shod hooves before setting out. The rags had long since come loose, but now the ground was so soft that our progress made no sound at all.

"She saved my wife's life," he said.

"You're married?" I squeaked.

Giving a snort, he said, "I was."

"Oh." I frowned. "Any children?"

"Two sons," he said. "Both lost to your father's wars."

"Oh," I said again. I'd known of the suffering my father's obsession had caused. I'd encountered it time and again during my 'tour' of the kingdom. But to have it presented so plainly and unexpectedly made guilt twist my already unsettled stomach. "I'm sorry."

"Not your fault," he said, as brusque as ever. Bringing the horse to a halt, he said, "It's too dark. I'll need to walk him from here."

"Should I dismount?"

"No need." He took a small lantern from a pack and lit it. It pushed back the surrounding darkness, but only a little. Tiny moths and bugs flitted around it, casting disproportionately large shadows.

Slowly, we made our way even deeper into the woods. If he was following a path, I couldn't see it. I could hear rustling all around us, but somehow, I wasn't afraid. I had my sword at my hip, was mounted on a large horse, and was being led by the best swordsman I knew. Even if we were attacked, I was confident we would survive.

"Would you mind very much telling me how Alcina saved your wife?" I asked, breaking the silence at last.

"Don't mind," he said. "After our second boy was born, my wife never regained her strength. Was seeming to waste away in front of me. As our sons grew up and left to fight, she kept getting weaker and weaker. Finally I went to the woods, five, six years ago I guess it was. I'd heard a witch lived there. I searched and searched, and eventually found an old woman and begged for her help. She charged me nothing, and after listening to my story, gave me some medicine, and bade me return for more if the weakness came back."

"The medicine helped?"

"It did. My wife grew strong again and thrived for a good half year. Eventually her health began to fail again, and I went back to the woods. The old woman was gone, but I found someone else living in her cottage, a younger woman. She told me she knew all about my wife's sickness and gave me more medicine. I went back five times in all, and each time she helped my wife and asked nothing in return." He sighed, his back bowing for a moment. "Then one morning my wife just… didn't awaken. She'd passed away during the night."

"I'm sorry," I said again.

"It was a blessing, in a way," he said. "She didn't live long enough to hear about the death of our second boy."

I sucked in a sharp breath. So much suffering. Alcina had helped where she could, while my father had condemned this man's sons to death. Witch or no, what clearer evidence was there that his way was wrong and hers was right?

"I returned to the woods and told her that my wife was gone," he said, his voice low. "I told her that the extra time she'd given us — not just the extra time, but the extra strength and health she'd given her so that she could enjoy that time — was worth more to me than rubies or gold. I told her that I had nothing of value I could give her except myself, but that I would serve her thenceforth without question."

"What did she say?" I murmured.

"She accepted my service," he said, his low voice rumbling in the night. "And I have served her ever since."

We plodded on, me atop the rocking, broad back of the horse, and he on foot. Neither of us spoke again until we came to a clearing, the center of which contained a small cottage and an overgrown garden. "Here we are," he said. "The witch's house."

He escorted me into the cottage and left me there, telling me he'd bring me a supply of meat in the morning. I'd only gotten a glimpse of the room from his lantern, but I'd seen where the bed was. All at once, exhaustion fell upon me, pressing me down with the weight of a mountain. Though I feared the bed would be covered in dust and possibly infested with bugs after all this time, I stumbled my way across the dark room, hands outstretched until I found it.

It didn't immediately make me sneeze, and I could feel nothing unpleasant when I pulled back the counterpane and slid my hand between the sheets, just ordinary fabric.

It was either the bed or the floor. I undid my boots and slid under the sheet. The sheer bliss of being able to lay down swamped everything else. The aches in my arms and legs, the turmoil in my mind and heart, none of them could keep me awake any longer. I sank into sleep between one breath and the next, and knew nothing more.

A breeze stirred my hair. My mind was still heavy with sleep, but I could tell that something was amiss. My room at the castle almost never had stray breezes; it was carefully insulated against the outside, with nary a crack to let in the night air. Sometimes in the winter the fire went out in the night and a draft came down the chimney flue, but it wasn't winter now, and the flue was always kept closed in the late spring and throughout the summer months.

I blinked open my eyes to bright sunlight and again felt

the curious breeze stroking across my cheeks and tugging at my hair. It took several long moments for me to remember where I was and why I was there.

"Alcina," I whispered.

What had I done? Caught up in the horror of her revelation about my father, I'd abandoned her to face him alone. Even if he was gone for now, when he returned, he would be furious. Furious and *dangerous*.

Throwing back the covers, I got to my feet and looked around.

This had to be Alcina's former home. I padded around on the smooth wooden floor and inspected the room. It felt surprisingly airy and fresh for a place that had been locked up for so long.

On one wall sat a large fireplace, swept clean. I checked the flue, but it was closed. It didn't even leave a trace of ash on my hands.

On either side of the fireplace shelves were built into the wall. They contained all manner of things: sachets of herbs tied with colorful ribbons like those I'd seen in Alcina's secret room, jars of substances both strange and recognizable, dried flowers hanging off the edges, folded stacks of cloth in various bright shades, beautifully carved boxes, large feathers and tiny ones, and what appeared to be a pile of small rocks. There were three gaps among the strange and varied items, as though things had been removed and never replaced, but no dust gathered in the empty spaces.

The scents of balsam and pine drifted from the shelf and mingled with those of cinnamon and ginger. I picked up one of the carved boxes and opened it, startling when a high, sweet tune began to pour out of it. Smiling, I shook my head and closed the box, cutting off the music, and replaced the box where I'd found it.

Everything was remarkably clean. I wondered if Alcina

had returned to the cottage to care for it, but even as the thought occurred to me, I found myself shaking my head again. She'd never been away from the castle—from me—for long enough to do so. At least, not in the past few years.

That persistent breeze swept over me again, chilling the back of my neck and making me shiver. Where was it coming from?

I turned and looked over the rest of the cottage. The wall opposite the fireplace was covered in more shelves, but these were weighed down with books, everything from loosely bound sheets of parchment to expensively sewn together and leather-bound tomes. Along the wall to my right, opposite the door, sat the small bed I'd slept on and a dresser with several drawers, one of them slightly crooked in the way of inexpertly-made furniture. I went over and pulled it out, jerking it open when it stuck. It was filled with clothing: simple and shapeless garments made of far coarser stuff than I'd ever worn. Even my practice clothes and the dress I'd borrowed from Esmerelda years ago had been of better, softer cloth than the plain homespun material of these. I rubbed the coarse cloth between my fingers, thinking of Alcina.

I closed the drawer with a shove and turned to finish my survey of the room. Across from me was the door as well as a stove and what looked to be a kitchen storage cupboard.

There were no windows, not even one paned with thin sheets of horn like those I had seen in some merchant's houses.

Yet I had awoken to sunlight, and the interior of the cottage was bright with a sourceless light, the pans hanging on the wall of the tiny kitchen area gleaming, the wooden floor shining.

A gust of air swept around me, spiraling down from the top of my head to my toes.

I swallowed dryly. "Hello?" I whispered.

A whisper came in response, brushing against my ear ticklishly and making me flinch. *"Welcome, welcome back."*

"I'm—" I hesitated, unsure how the... current tenant?... tenants?... would react if they knew I wasn't Alcina. Would they grow angry? Would they attack me?

Better to know now than to try to fool them and slip up later. Besides, I was going to return to the castle soon anyway. I couldn't leave Alcina alone there. "I'm not the—the person who lived here before."

The wind died down, then swirled up again. It didn't seem violent, but agitated. It blew in my face. *"You wear the token."*

"The token?"

There was a confusing tug at the back of my neck. It took me a moment to remember the events of the previous night— was it only the previous night? It felt as though it had been days ago. My hand went to the necklace I'd tucked beneath my clothes. Pulling it out, I examined it as I hadn't had time to do before.

From a silver chain a locket in the shape of an oval slowly spun to and fro. It was similar to one I'd had when I was child. Mine had contained a tiny painting of my mother, but I'd lost it when I'd 'accidentally' fallen in a river. My lips quirked at the memory. I'd been sad to lose the locket, but I'd been allowed swimming lessons, which had been the point of the accident. I wondered if this locket also contained an image. I longed to open it and see, but that would mean breaking a promise to Alcina, and that I would not do.

Holding up the locket on the chain, I said, "Is this the token?"

A tiny breath of wind made it spin faster, flashing in the sourceless light. *"Yes. Her token."*

"She gave it to me," I said, quickly adding, "She will come here herself when she can." *She promised.*

There was a moment of thoughtful stillness. *"You may stay,"* the wind whispered in my ear. I felt my shoulders loosen in relief.

"Thank you." I tucked the locket back under my clothes. "What should I call you? Do you have a name?"

The breeze gusted against my cheek. *"I am Spirit of Wind,"* came the voiceless reply.

A spirit! I'd known it must be, but hearing it made it real. I tensed as nursery stories swirled through my memory. Spirits could be tricksters or helpers, depending on their whim of the moment, but most stories warned against them. I'd quickly grown out of believing in them. They'd seemed merely convenient props upon which to hang morality tales, no more real than talking animals. How wrong I'd been. Would I encounter a talking cat next?

There could be dire consequences for rudeness, or so the stories taught. I reminded myself that surely Alcina would not have sent me into danger.

"I'm honored to meet you, Spirit of Wind." The breeze stirred and gently tugged at my hair. "Is there," I looked around the windowless room, "Could there also be a Spirit of Light here?" In a soundless reply, the cottage faded into darkness, then brightened again. "It's nice to meet you as well," I said, and automatically dropped into a curtsey.

Puffs of air against my cheeks made me think of laughter.

Straightening, I looked around the cottage again. "Are there more of you?" I asked, trying not to sound nervous.

"Yes," the wind hissed into my ear. *"There are more."*

I waited, but no further explanation seemed to be forthcoming. "I would meet them," I said tentatively, but there was no response save another teasing flurry that quickly abated. After a moment of waiting, I decided to explore a little more rather than demand an introduction and risk rudeness.

The light was dimming slightly, and I wondered at it until I heard the sound of tapping against the roof, first a few individual sounds, then more and more. Going to the door, I opened it to find the rain pouring down. I thought of Gregory stuck out in the deluge, and shivered.

As though my thoughts had summoned him, he appeared from the edge of the forest, leading his horse with a burden on her back. It wasn't until he neared the cottage that I saw that it was the corpse of a deer.

"I have brought you meat," he called to me, coming to a halt in front of my door.

"Thank you," I said. I turned to the cottage and spoke to the air. "May I invite a guest?"

The rain drove harder against the side of the house for a moment. Then the whisper came, *"We know him. He may enter."* The way the spirit said the words reminded me of a child at play, pretending to be grand.

"Please come inside and get dry and warm," I said. Something nagged at me — though there was still no fire in the grate, the air inside was warmer than the air blowing in through the open door. Another spirit's doing?

"I can only stay for a little time," he said, but dismounted and heaved the deer off his saddle. "I must bring back the doe's heart, but you are welcome to the rest."

It was a good thing I'd learned how to preserve meat, both from my time spent in the palace kitchens and from discussing it with the butcher. Salted and dried, I would have enough to last me for some time.

Except, I reminded myself, I wouldn't be staying.

"Why do you need her heart?" I asked.

"Alcina bade me bring her the heart of a doe," he said. "I know not why, nor did I ask." His tone implied that I shouldn't, either.

"You must take me back to Alcina," I said. "I was not in

my right mind when I agreed to leave."

He shook his head. "I obey her," he said.

"I am your princess!"

His swarthy face crinkled as he smiled. He pushed his iron-gray hair out of his eyes and said, "She is the queen. But even if she were not, I would obey her."

"But she will be in danger," I pleaded. "When my father returns—"

"She is a clever woman. Trust her," he said, and I closed my mouth.

I did trust her. Nevertheless, I feared for her.

"She said that she will send word when she can," he said. "In the meantime, wait for her. Trust her," he said again.

"Very well," I said, though it went against every instinct. I wanted nothing more than to protect her, to be the one she could turn to and rely upon. Instead, I was still relying on her, leaving her to face danger while I fled and hid. I hated it, and hated myself for agreeing to it, but now that it was done, turning back could well make things worse. "I will be awaiting word from her. Please tell her that."

"I shall."

Chapter 5

True to his word, Gregory didn't stay long. The gray light gave little indication as to time, but it was likely not even noon when the rain began to let up and my swordmaster took his leave. He left me with a slaughtered deer (sans heart), a mysterious cottage inhabited by strange spirits, and absolutely no idea where I was or how to find my way home.

It was both freeing and terrifying.

I'd been surrounded by people my entire life. I was awoken by servants each morning and tucked in by them each night. And though I'd done the work of a servant at various times — cleaning, cooking, and doing all manner of domestic chores, some less pleasant than others — I'd never had to do *everything* for myself.

Nor did I have to now, I soon learned.

My swordmaster had refused anything to eat or drink, but once he was gone, I realized how hungry I was. Investigating the cupboard in the kitchen, I discovered supplies of grains and some dried fruit. Enough to make a simple porridge and take the edge off my hunger. There was even a barrel filled with water that smelled surprisingly fresh.

What I didn't find was any firewood.

I stood in front of the stove, pot filled with water, grains at the ready, and frowned. Finally, I spoke aloud. "Spirit of Wind," I called. A stirring of air greeted me in reply. "Is one of the spirits here a Spirit of Heat?"

"*Spirit of Warmth,*" the breeze corrected me.

I nodded. "Spirit of Warmth," I called in no particular direction, "I greet you." Perhaps it was my imagination, but the air around my hands seemed to grow hotter.

Dared I ask favors from the spirits? The Spirit of Light seemed to reflect the light outside without being asked, making the cottage brighter when the sun was out and dimmer when the sky was covered by clouds. Had Alcina asked it to do so, or was it acting on its own whim?

There was no firewood to be found, and the hearth had been far too clean. This might be the Spirits' domain and I merely a trespasser, but the cottage had been built for a human's use.

"Spirit of Warmth," I said, my heart in my throat, "Would you be willing to heat the stove for me?"

There was no reply, but I felt the metal in front of me quickly grow warm, then hot. I placed the pot on it. "Thank you," I said. "If you please, continue to warm it like this until the pot begins to boil."

The spirit must have understood, because the stove remained hot, glowing a cheery red, as I finished preparing my late breakfast. When it was complete, I removed the pot from the stove and said, "I am grateful, Spirit of Warmth. Please stop heating the stove now." A few minutes later, the stove was merely warm to the touch, and soon cooled completely.

Should I collect some firewood for future use? Or would that be impolite, as though I didn't think the Spirit of Warmth was up to the task?

I bit my lip and decided to wait. The weather was growing warmer at this time of year, and if the Spirit grew capricious and left me in the cold, I would be uncomfortable, but I wouldn't freeze to death overnight.

My hands moved automatically to clean the pot and spoon I'd used and place them back where I'd found them. I considered exploring the forest around the cottage, but the gray quality to the light and the sound of the rain starting up again dissuaded me. Very soon I would need to clean the doe and find a place to hang the meat to dry, but it could wait a little while longer.

I stood in the middle of the room and looked around, feeling at a loss. My days were always so full, with lessons, practice, and Alcina's assignments. It was vanishingly rare that I had time like this, without obligations of any kind.

I wandered around the small room, coming to a halt in front of the bookshelf across from the fireplace.

At the castle, Alcina had had a smaller shelf of books in her chamber, and I remembered the ones stacked on the table in her secret room. But there were far more here than I'd ever seen at once. When I picked a few up and began paging through them, I discovered a rough sort of organization to them.

The first section of the shelf contained books about herbs and medicines. There weren't many of these books, four in total, two of which were the same: an old version, its pages fragile and crumbling, and a new one copied out in Alcina's hand. Her writing had never been beautiful, not for as long as I'd known her. It was cramped and slightly awkward, but it was readable. Her version contained additional notations and thoughts, and I found myself leaning against the wall and eventually settling to the floor as I read page after page in that dear, beloved script.

There was something vaguely familiar about these books, not just the writing but the content itself. As I read through the instructions on how to make tinctures and healing broths, it dawned on me that they were *recipes*, not so different from the ones I'd learned from the cook. One part root, two parts water, a pinch of salt—it could have been a recipe for soup. Except these 'soups' could do all sorts of things…maybe even save someone's life.

Halfway through the thin volume I came across the concoction Alcina had made for Gregory's wife, one of several labeled "For the restoration of vitality". Alcina had kept detailed notes, with descriptions of the woman's symptoms and what her husband had said about her reactions to the medicine.

I began to see what Alcina had meant when she'd talked about 'True magic'. True magic was the spirits of Wind and Light and Warmth that flitted about the cottage unseen. True magic was the mirror in her secret room, which had shown me things it still turned my stomach to think about.

But this, these recipes, anyone could make them. Well, perhaps not anyone — there was a trick to properly chopping and mixing and boiling things for the right amount of time, as I'd learned in the castle kitchens — but anyone could be *taught* to make these. They weren't magical, or perhaps they were, but certainly not in the same way that the spirits were.

Eventually I returned the book to the shelf, reluctantly running my fingers along its spine before pulling my hand away.

The next section of books was a surprise: tales of true love and passion, endlessly reimagined plots that all told essentially the same story: two people finding each other, falling in love, and living happily ever after.

I puzzled over these. They didn't have notations the way the books about herb usage did, nor were they in Alcina's hand. Yet they were clearly well-read. At first I wondered if they'd been a gift from some grateful person she'd helped, but there were too many and of too great a variety for that. Eventually I realized that she must simply enjoy reading them.

Apparently Alcina was a romantic at heart.

As I set another book back on the shelf, I noticed that the sound of rain had long since stopped and that the quality of the light had changed, becoming golden.

I would look over the rest of the books later. Sighing, I

stretched and went to see about the deer. Fortunately, there was a large box of salt in the pantry.

It was the next day that I found the treasure.

I spent what was left of the previous day preserving some of the deer meat, my efforts inexpert but adequate. Then, with the kind help of the Spirit of Warmth, I turned a portion of the remainder into a hearty stew. As the sun set I'd followed the sound of water until I found a small stream that ran nearby, cold but clear. I washed thoroughly in the dimming light before hurrying back into the cottage and curling into bed that evening, shivering. The blankets seemed to heat around me, cocooning me in warmth, and I smiled and spoke aloud to thank the Spirit of Warmth.

"Just wait," came a whisper in my ear, sending chills down the back of my neck. *"Come summer I'll be the one you're blessing. You won't want the Spirit of Warmth around at all."*

I laughed a little and pulled the blanket around me more tightly. "I'll always want both of you around," I said impulsively. That gave me pause. *Did* I want such dangerous, capricious friends?

There was a light touch on my cheek, like the brush of a kiss. I felt my mouth stretch into a smile again and my eyes drift closed.

Yes, I realized. I did want them around. I wanted their friendship, and not merely for the sake of convenience.

When I awoke the next day, it was to the sound of more rain. After a breakfast of stew, I returned to the bookshelf. I hesitated over the romantic stories. If Alcina had really read and enjoyed these, perhaps I could learn more about her by reading them as well. I could not have said why it was so important to me to understand her better. I knew only that I wished to.

My hand hovered over the well-read novels, then passed on. There would be time enough later, and I wanted to know what other secrets the bookshelf might hold. A few almost untouched books stood out to me, proving to be cookbooks when I investigated. I smiled as I paged through them, and wondered if Alcina didn't like to cook. I still hadn't had a chance to make a meal for her. If she'd allowed it, I would have liked to cook for her every day.

As I was replacing the last of these recipe books I felt something behind it, preventing me from pushing the book in all the way. Pulling it back out, I found a smaller book wedged against the back of the shelf. It looked as though it had slid down behind it accidentally. I extracted it, expecting another recipe book.

Well, I have escaped, the first page began. I recognized Alcina's hand, though it seemed both more and less neat — still cramped, but as though the writer was making an effort for it not to be so. At the same time, there was a rough, unpracticed quality to it.

I kept reading.

I can hardly believe it. I was certain I would die in that house along with my mother, may her soul find the peace she was denied in life.

Frea — the woman who found me and took me in told me I should call her that — said that I might tame my thoughts by writing them. She said she is not used to hearing so many words at once, and bade me write them first before speaking them, choosing only what is most important to say aloud. She said that it doesn't matter exactly what I write, and that it need not mean anything to anyone except for me. In fact, it need not mean anything even to me.

So I am writing in the book she gave me. If nothing else, it is good practice.

She says her True name isn't Frea. She told me that I should not tell anyone my True name, for it will give others Power over me. I'm not sure if I believe her or not.

It doesn't matter if I believe her, though. She saved me, and is letting me stay with her, and she says she will teach me. At first I feared that she would make me leave. She tried to convince me that being a witch is a hard life. But when I explained that I truly have nowhere to go, she said I could stay.

I took a hard breath, and another. Alcina had written a date on the corner of that first entry. After a moment of calculation, I realized that she'd been seventeen when she'd written this first entry. The same age I'd been when I'd first met her two years later. And…I was nineteen now, the same age *she'd* been when we'd met. It made me a little dizzy to think of it, that I was now just as old as that woman who'd seemed so untouchable and cool. The gap between us had seemed tremendous then. But that was before I'd come to know her.

Carefully, reverently, I set the book on the dresser next to the bed. I had not expected to find such a treasure, and though I craved more, I decided to wait. I would read a little at a time, learning about Alcina's past as I went.

It did not occur to me that I shouldn't read Alcina's private thoughts. We had shared each other's space for years, each becoming the other's friend and confidant. I left the book and went back to the bookshelf.

The remainder of the titles were less organized. Three religious tomes sat together. Like the recipe books, they looked almost untouched. One book detailed the history of our kingdom, and another of our neighboring kingdom, the one where Prince Karl would someday rule. I set both of them aside to read later. I would try to keep up with my studies even when Alcina wasn't there to teach and direct me. I probably already knew the information from both history books, but at the very least, I could review it and keep it fresh in my mind. I hoped to make Alcina proud when I saw her again.

An obvious gap stood out on the second shelf, and I puzzled over it for some time until I realized that Alcina's books on True magic must have once occupied that space. She had likely brought them with her and kept them in her secret room. I could even visualize the small stack I'd seen there, imagining them fitting into the empty spot. I wondered why she hadn't brought her books on herbs with her as well. Perhaps her space had been limited when she traveled to the palace. Perhaps she'd memorized the contents.

Perhaps she'd hoped to return here.

I found little else on the shelves until, inspired by the discovery of Alcina's diary, I checked behind the rest of the titles. There, wedged at the bottom near the floor, I discovered three more books, small, plain, handbound things that I thought at first were more diaries.

But no, they were something else entirely.

Chapter 6

The new books I'd discovered were not written in Alcina's hand, thankfully. I don't know what I would have done if they had been: they were books about marital relations…that is, what two people might do to give each other pleasure. Not intended for titillation, but for education and explanation.

Just the first few pages made me gasp, shocked. They sent strange feelings surging through me, making my face heat from more than just embarrassment. I slammed the book shut and was ready to shove it back behind the shelf, but then I hesitated, looking around furtively.

The only ones here were the spirits and myself, and I was certain that the spirits had little care for such things as human books…or human bodies. I was in the depths of a forest, quite alone. And — and Alcina *must* have read these books. She must know what they said. I imagined her sitting on the bed, turning the pages. Would she have retained her calm, cool demeanor? Or would she have found herself blushing as I was, strange tingles surging through her chest and between her legs?

I closed my eyes and gave my head a shake. It wasn't seemly for me to think of her in such a way.

I took the books anyway, and settled onto the bed.

The first book described what a man might do to give a woman pleasure, as well as the other way around. I found myself more intrigued by the former than the latter, studying the simple ink sketches closely. Never had I found a source of such information, presented with such blunt and frank language. It explained, too, what one might do if one wished for a child, and what one might do if one *didn't*. I read it from beginning to end, paying more attention to some parts than others. My whole body felt strangely alive, my skin hungry for the touches I'd just read about.

The second book was even more of a surprise. I opened it and began to skim, expecting it to be more of the same, perhaps more advanced techniques. This book, though, described what two *men* might do together.

Among the nations in our part of the world, our kingdom was unique. A few years before my mother had died, the king had declared that men could marry men and women could marry women. Though none of my scholarly teachers had outright said so, I'd picked up on their feelings about the idea: ambivalent at best, disgusted at worst.

When I'd discussed it with Alcina, she'd told me that my mother had once had a brother she'd loved dearly, and he had in turn had a beloved he wished to wed. She'd asked my father to make it possible, and he'd agreed.

Thinking back upon it, I wondered how Alcina had known of my uncle. Had my father told her of it? Or had she discovered something in the records or a journal of his, like the diary of hers I'd found? More likely it was common knowledge, and my teachers had simply never thought it important enough to tell me.

"Both your uncle and his husband died in your father's wars when you were still very young," Alcina had said when I asked after them, her voice gentle. "I'm not surprised you don't remember them."

I could not mourn for two men I had never met, but I mourned for them the way I had when I'd grown old enough to understand my mother's demise: for the missed opportunity to know them.

My eyes returned to the book in my hand. Perhaps because of the reluctance of my tutors, the idea of two men or two women together always left me a little uncomfortable. Still, I began paging through the book, finding myself flooded with new information on topics I'd never given much thought to.

A few pages in, I abruptly set the book aside. I'd had a sudden suspicion about what the third book might contain.

I let it fall open and stared down at the pages, my heart pounding.

I was right.

The third book was about what two women could do together.

Images of Alcina came to me irresistibly as I read. Her lovely face, her beautiful body, covered only by a thin nightdress as she prepared for sleep. I imagined her touching me, but more than that, I imagined touching *her*. I couldn't help it. I couldn't *stop*. Every new page, each illustration, more graphic and explicit than the last, made me shift, made my body clench hungrily in ways that felt strange and new.

Squeezing my eyes shut, I let the book fall from my hands onto the bed. I clapped my hands to my cheeks, but the sting did nothing to shake the images from my mind. With my eyes closed, my hands became Alcina's in my mind. Except that she would never slap me. She had always touched me gently.

A flash of memory hit me: helping Alcina with her hair, pulling it back and tucking it behind the shell of her delicate ear. She'd gone so still under my hands. Now my fingers (her fingers) trailed over my cheeks and around the curves of my own ears. Strange shivers trickled down the back of my neck.

I'd helped Alcina remove the earrings she wore for court each day, unclasping the jeweled and heavy things and putting them away in the ornate jewelry box. Now I traced down to the lobe, first of one ear, then the other. A prickling awareness washed through me, making me shudder.

My fingers drifted around my neck and collarbones as I recalled undoing the clasp of her necklaces, the gems glittering as they caught the evening candlelight. She'd always cupped both hands around the back of her neck afterward, tilting her head forward and rocking it from side to side. I imitated the memory, pressing my fingers to the back of my neck and rolling my head. Then, deliberately, I lightened my touch. I let my fingers splay and skimmed them around to the front.

A tremor shook me, a gasp coming to my lips. It was as though my body was coming alive in a way it never had before. I'd reveled in the opportunities to push my physical limits, to tire myself out with swordwork or even the labor I'd had to undertake when Alcina had me play at being a servant. But this was something new.

Opening my eyes, I picked up the book from where I'd let it fall. The pages seemed to come alive, the crude (in every sense) drawings becoming intriguing when Alcina and I overlaid the women on the pages. The straightforward instructions somehow left me breathless.

In a dim corner of my mind I knew I should be cringing away from these thoughts. Alcina was my stepmother. I should be awash in guilt imagining her like this. I should be drowning in shame for imagining myself as her partner.

But I was alone, with only the spirits for company, and somehow I didn't mind if they saw me like this. What did they know of human thoughts, human shame? Bodiless themselves, how would they even begin to grasp what it was to touch or embrace?

I turned the page, drinking in the image of one woman with her mouth on the other woman's breast. Would that really feel...good?

Taking a breath, I yanked off my top and looked down at myself. My chest was pale, untouched by the sun, but my nipples were darker, a light brown. They were tightening as they always did when I removed my top, puckering slightly, their tips flushing redder.

What would Alcina's nipples look like? Her breasts were a little larger than mine, suited to her taller frame. They looked as though they would be soft. I let a finger brush over the tip of my right nipple. Sensation shot through me, pooling in my stomach and echoing between my legs. I bit my lip and squirmed.

If Alcina were to touch me like this — a jolt went through me, my breath catching. I could see her long fingers tracing over my nipple. Using her thumb and forefinger, she lightly pinched and rolled it. It tightened even further.

My sword callouses were rough against my skin, breaking the illusion. I frowned and cast about for a substitute, finally replacing Alcina's hands with Prince Karl's, larger than mine and almost as calloused.

I felt my face folding into a confused scowl as revulsion rose in my chest and my fingers stilled. I didn't want Prince Karl's hands. I wanted *Alcina's*, with her smooth skin and delicate nails. And I wanted *her* under my own sword-calloused fingers.

Would her body react the same way as mine?

I moved to my left nipple, as yet untouched and so not as puckered as its twin. My calloused fingers made sense if *I* was the one doing the touching. If it was Alcina's breasts under my hands. Perhaps after I'd helped her undress for the night. I teased her breasts, playing with them, moving my hands both in tandem and separately. Little bolts of lightning seemed to leap through my body and down between my legs. Would it be the same for her? Would she shift and bite her lip, unable to keep her body still? Would her breath stutter and her nipples tighten for me?

The thought made something sing through me. I squeezed my eyes shut again, being rougher with myself now, rougher than I would ever be with her, pinching and flicking until I was gasping.

I wanted—I wanted something. I wanted *Alcina*. Grabbing the book, I flipped the page. The woman had her mouth between her lover's legs.

Even having seen such things in the other books, it was hard to believe what I was seeing. Did people really *do* such things? Surely it would be…very unpleasant for the person doing it?

Almost without thinking about it, I slid my hand down over the fabric between my legs. As I pressed against my mound, a startled sound escaped my throat. My hips jerked up, and I found myself grinding up into the heel of my hand as shocks of sensation surged out from the point of contact.

I stopped before I could rub myself raw against the fabric. My chest was heaving, my eyes wide, staring at nothing.

Slowly, I pulled off the rest of my clothes, leaving myself bare. The room was warm, the light still gray. I looked down at the dark hair between my legs. Suddenly shy, I closed my eyes again.

A vision came to me. Alcina, in her nightdress. She wrapped her arms around me from behind and pressed her lips to the back of my neck. I reached up and stroked two fingers across my nape in a poor imitation of a kiss. "Alcina," I mumbled. "Alcina, Alcina." Her fingers slid to trail over my lips, which parted for them so that she could touch the tip of my tongue with them. They tasted faintly of salt. I closed my mouth on them and sucked for a moment before she pulled them away with a faint 'pop'.

What now?

Her hand slid down again, pressing between my legs, this time without the barrier of the fabric. I couldn't keep it away. But a mouth wouldn't feel like that, wouldn't just be pressure. Using two fingers, damp with spit, I swept them down through the triangle of dark hair until they reached the apex, and then even further.

Oh. *Oh*, that was so strange. My body twisted and froze and twisted again, uncertain whether or not it liked the light touch. It was...good? But different, so different. I teased against the nub of flesh there, a spot I'd never given any thought to and which now consumed my entire awareness.

If it wasn't my fingers, if it was a tongue, how would it feel? I stroked my tongue along the roof of my mouth, but it just left a ticklish trail in its wake. My fingers moved lightly up and down, then more firmly. My legs spread wide of their own accord, leaving me exposed and helpless.

Alcina would *never* touch me like this. But what if I could touch her, if I could tease her, letting my fingers slide between her legs, just two fingers rubbing over and over that place that felt so strange but somehow so irresistible? Even if she squeezed her legs together, she wouldn't be able to stop me from slipping into the crevice between them. My own legs squeezed together, and it was even better, my body folded around my increasingly frantic fingers.

"Alcina," I groaned aloud, startling myself.

Writhing, panting, I pushed up into my own touch even as my mind filled with Alcina. If only I could do this to her, *for* her. Give her this, this building sensation, unbearably good. Sweat was gathering on the back of my neck and under my arms. It felt like fighting, in a way. I drove my body toward the unknown end. My other hand went to my nipples again, pinching them in turn, and that made it even better, magnifying every sensation.

My hips stuttered, my whole body seeming to clench in on itself. A whimper escaped my throat. I arched off the bed, my legs parting and squeezing together again. I felt like a tree shaken by a violent storm, torn this way and that until finally the tremors calmed again.

Slowly, slowly the excitement faded, leaving me exhausted. I wiped my hands on the sheets, uncaring; I would have to wash the linens after this anyway. Lassitude filled me. I lay there a long time. I don't remember what I thought about.

Eventually ordinary hunger and a need to relieve myself forced me to sit up again. When I did so I found that the third volume had been shoved to the side, fortunately not crushed when I'd flopped back. I picked it up and it fell open to the same page as before: one woman lay back, her legs splayed open. A second woman had her head between her legs. The first woman's head was tossed back, her mouth open, her eyes closed.

A pulse of heat surged through me, making my body twitch and clench again. And with the sensation came another vision: Alcina's body spread for me to feast on, her head thrown back in ecstasy. My fingers, my tongue on that tiny, secret place between her legs.

The book fell from my grasp back onto the bed as I buried my face in my hands.

I loved her. That was not a surprise. I'd loved her for almost as long as I'd known her.

But I didn't just love her. I *wanted* her.

Not as my stepmother. Not just as my companion. As my lover. I wanted to scatter kisses across her face and throat. I wanted to bring her such pleasure, to keep going until her facade shattered, until her skin was flushed and sweating, her body eager and open and as hungry for mine as mine was for her.

It was impossible. She was my stepmother! She'd always treated me with gentle warmth, but never, *never* anything like this. Nothing even close.

But what if. What if she did feel the same? It wasn't as though she could have shown it. She was far too good to do so.

I thought of all the time we'd spent together, of how I

always set my chair next to hers, of how she'd let me lean into her. Of how she'd let me braid her hair when preparing for bed, and offered to braid mine. Of how she'd told me that she was glad she'd met me. How she'd been lonely and hadn't even realized it.

Was it possible...?

No. I didn't dare to hope. To be wrong would be more than just painful — it could be disastrous if I said or did the wrong thing. My father was already convinced she'd ensnared me. How much worse would it be if he knew of my desire for her? And Alcina herself, would she react with anger? Shame? Disgust? The thought of her eyes softening with pity sent a shudder of revulsion through me.

I could not let her know. I could not.

But what if. What if?

Lifting my head, I swallowed hard and blinked away the burning in my eyes. I was, first and foremost, a princess. My duty was to my kingdom. My own joy, my own pleasure, were secondary to that.

Alcina was married to my father. My stomach twisted as I realized that they had very likely done many of the things listed in the first volume, but I forced myself to acknowledge it. They were married. Even if Alcina did feel the same way for me as I did about her, even if she had not been my stepmother, even if she desired women, desired *me*, I knew she would not betray her husband.

She kept her promises.

I rose to my feet and gathered the three books I'd discovered. Carefully, I tucked them behind the other volumes where I'd first found them. Then I went outside to bathe in the cold stream and tried to drive all thoughts of Alcina's body from my mind.

It worked.

For a little while.

Chapter 7

The writing on the next entry in the journal was a little neater, a little less uncertain.

We were never poor. It might have been easier if we were.

My father is a fabric merchant. He's away for long stretches, selling his wares around the kingdom and negotiating with the weavers for more.

Alcina had always spoken to tailors with authority and surety. Of course, she'd spoken to everyone with quiet confidence. But I remembered the way she would rub the edge of a piece of fabric between two fingers before nodding or shaking her head. I remembered the respect in the eyes of the tailors who watched her and agreed with her.

We had enough to live on and some to spare. Enough for my father to drink as much as he pleased as often as he pleased.

For years I didn't understand what he did to my mother. She managed to shield me from the worst of it. Despite that, I was always afraid of him.

When he returned from one of his trips and told her he'd met someone else, she raised her voice for the only time in my memory. He killed her that night, and I fled, making my way blindly out of the town and into the forest.

As far as I know he still lives, along with his new wife and child. If he has not yet killed her too.

I was shaking so hard that the words were blurring. Not with grief or pity, but with *rage*. Oh, how I wanted to hurt the man who'd frightened my Alcina. I wanted to slice him open with my sword. No, I wanted to strangle him with my bare hands.

I turned the page.

Living with Frea is very good. She is still quite sharp, despite her age. She has set me to re-copying some of her books, giving me additions to make as I go. I have come up with a few ideas of my own, some of which she thought worth including.

I could sense the quiet pride beneath her straightforward words.

There is something very strange about living here. Light fills the cottage even though there are no windows. Frea often whispers as though to herself, but when she does so the stove will grow hot of its own accord. The air stirs even when the door is closed. When I asked Frea about it, she said that it is True Magic, and that she will teach me the secret of it someday.

That made me smile. I knew what, or rather who, Frea had been speaking to.

If only I'd been able to meet the old woman. But she hadn't been here when I arrived, and probably not for some time before that. She was surely gone.

For three days, the rain remained a steady drum beat on the roof. I explored the cottage thoroughly, eventually finding a small, cool basement hidden beneath the floorboards. There was also a separate shed, empty but for a long table that reminded me of the one in Alcina's secret room back in the castle. It was there that I cured the remaining deer meat and hung it to dry, hoping that Alcina would not object too strongly that I'd used her workroom for such a purpose when she eventually joined me. As she must. As she promised.

I avoided the books on... marital relations.

My feelings were tangled. Guilt and shame mingled with excitement and hunger. The oddest part was that the guilt wasn't because I desired Alcina. Alcina was so beautiful. Surely anyone would feel the same if they knew her as I did. How could anyone resist someone as kind, as lovely, as warm as she?

But I knew I *shouldn't* feel the way I did, the warmth of friendship having ignited into desire. She was my stepmother. I shouldn't want to touch her. I shouldn't want to see her face twisted in pleasure. I shouldn't want—

I knew I should feel guilty about my desire, but I felt worse because of my lack of guilt. What was wrong with me, that I could feel such things and not care?

So I pushed it all from my mind. During those three days of rain I cured the deer meat, and when I wasn't doing that, I chose from the histories, the books on medicine, and the recipe books. I tried to keep my mind on them, even as it wandered off on its own into thoughts of Alcina. Whenever I caught myself getting distracted or tempted to look at *those* books again, I would firmly turn my thoughts back to what I was reading, or get up and walk around the small room, or even, once, go stand out in the rain until I was soaked and shivering.

To my relief, on the fourth day after I arrived the sun finally came out, steady in a cloudless sky. I stepped outside in my bare feet, relishing the warmth and turning my face to it as I drew in deep breaths of the grass-scented air.

"*Morning morning morning,*" the Spirit of Wind sang in my ear, though whether it was a greeting or simply an observation I didn't know.

"Good morning," I replied.

Wind shook through the pine needles of a nearby stand of trees, sending a cascade of droplets flashing in the sun. I grinned at the spirit's antics, the trees too far to splash me. The grass was soft under my feet, and I found myself strolling around the house, soaking in the sunlight.

The long grass brushed ticklishly at my ankles. As I rounded the side of the house, I found an overgrown tangle, with vines winding this way and that through what must have once been a carefully-tended garden. I took a step closer, trying to identify what kind of plant had taken over. As I gently moved them aside, I blinked down at the sight that greeted me.

I knew those feathery green bunches. Those were certainly carrots. And those, those were radishes!

Crouching down, I took hold of one of the bunches of stalks and pulled. The root held for a moment, then came free all at once, nearly sending me backwards into the wet grass. When I regained my balance, I stared at the carrot. It was large and deep in color, surprisingly free of blemishes or the ravages of insects or worms. Once I'd rinsed the dirt off, it would make a fine supplement to my next meal.

I pulled up a radish next, and found it to be just as beautiful as the carrot, if not moreso. The bright red seemed almost too good to be real.

As I let the vine settle back in place, I realized that pods dangled from it, ripe and plump. Plucking one of them, I slit it open with my thumbnail. Rich green peas filled it in a neat line, just the right ripeness for picking and eating.

Insects and fungi were some of the biggest threats to a farmer's crops, I'd learned, though drought and early frost could be even worse. It was more than surprising to find such a bounty nearly untouched, especially after several years of neglect. At the very least, the birds and animals of the forest should have discovered it.

Crouching next to the garden, I sat back on my heels and narrowed my eyes, looking at the carrot I'd pulled, marveling at how perfect it was in both color and shape. Rising, I took it to the stream to wash it, then took a bite. It was crisp and sweet, its flavor strong and as perfect as everything else about it. Looking up, I called, "Spirit of Wind?"

"*Yess?*" The hiss tickled my ear, making me shake my head hard.

"Is there a Spirit of — of Growth that helps with the garden?"

"*Vitality,*" came the answer after a moment of what seemed to be hesitation. The spirit was strangely subdued.

"Vitality?" I echoed.

"*She brought it. But it couldn't help,*" there was a petulant quality to the words, like an angry child. "*It grows the garden but it couldn't help.*"

"Couldn't help? Help with what?"

Air rippled against my face, but there was no reply.

I have discovered the secret!

Frea went out to the garden today. Usually I help her, but I awoke with my head hurting and my body too cold. She bade me stay in bed and brewed me one of her bitter teas to drink. I tossed and turned for a time, before I started feeling too hot where before I'd been chilled. Tossing off the blankets, I cried aloud, "It's hot!"

Something whispered to me, "I can cool you."

I nearly jumped out of my skin. "Who are you?"

It said it was a Spirit of Wind and blew across my skin, making me shiver and laugh. It was like a child, playful and self-serving by turns.

There are three of them in all: Spirits of Light, of Warmth, and of Wind.

When Frea returned, I told her smugly that I had learned the truth. She did not seem surprised, but studied me carefully. "They do not frighten you?"

"Should they?"

"No, but some people are afraid of that which they can't understand or control," she said. Smiling, she patted my head. "You are a good girl."

Three spirits. But the Spirit of Wind had said there was a fourth, of Vitality, and the improbably perfect vegetables certainly seemed magical. Had the Spirit of Wind lied? To Alcina, or to me? Had Alcina misunderstood? Had I?

I frowned and closed the book, setting it aside. The air was bright with sunshine. It had been a week since I'd arrived, and today I was going to explore the forest around the cottage.

Putting on one of the coarse tunics from the drawer and the boots I'd brought with me, I made my way into the forest. I moved slowly, frequently pausing to look around and get my bearings. I made marks of my passage, breaking off small branches and scratching lines into the bark of trees. If I got lost, no one would come looking for me.

Or would they? Would the spirits seek me out if I didn't return? Had they sought for Alcina after she'd left? Had she told them that she wouldn't be back? I wondered if she'd ever expected to return.

A breathless pain gathered in my chest when I thought of her. She'd been so certain that my father would kill her when she became inconvenient. It wasn't surprising, given her history. And she'd been right. I shuddered at the memory of my father's face and took a hard breath, forcing my thoughts back to the present.

If I asked the Spirit of Light to help me find my way in the woods, or the Spirit of Warmth to keep me from getting a chill as I traveled, or the Spirit of Wind to keep me company, I wondered, would they? Could they, or were they tied to the cottage? Were they prisoners, or there by choice?

I wished Alcina were there to ask. I wished she were there for a lot of reasons. I missed her companionship, her gentle guidance, her thoughtful conversations. I missed her touch, a hand against my cheek, fingers stroking over my hair.

That was dangerous territory. I wasn't going to think about *that*, I reminded myself, and firmly turned my thoughts back to the path ahead of me. I needed to be able to find my way back, not lose myself in useless circles of longing.

Frea summoned the Spirits herself, I read the next day, almost as though Alcina were answering one of the questions I could not put to her.

She has lived here since she was my age, or perhaps even younger. I asked if she'd had a mentor like she is to me, but she said she had not. She learned everything from books, and from things she heard from the people she helped, and from trial and error. She found the cottage abandoned and overgrown, and fixed it with the help of her brother, who left her afterward and returned to the village.

I wondered if Frea's brother was still alive, still out there somewhere.

Summoning spirits was one of the things she learned from a book, she told me. She'd helped an old man whose stomach pained him, brewing tea that eased his suffering. In gratitude, he presented her with all the books he owned. She said the others were of little interest, but one of them was a book about True Magic, and how one might summon spirits to help or guide, in exchange for giving them a place to stay.

I asked why everyone didn't do so, and she smiled at me and patted my head. "There is always a risk in such things," she told me. "If the spirit should begin to feel trapped or unappreciated, it might well turn upon the one who summoned it. It might sour the milk or knock down the firewood, or do worse, like stirring the air around a candle flame until it sets the curtains on fire."

"But if the one who summoned it treats it with respect," I said nervously, "then it will not do such things?"

"Not to the one who summoned it, no," she said. "But it can take offense on behalf of those it likes, too. If it felt that someone was a threat or unkind to one that it considered a friend, it might play such pranks on the one it disliked."

I understood, then. Such spirits would be dangerous in a village or town with people living close to each other. Dangerous for the villagers, but dangerous for the reputation of the one who'd summoned them, too, who would be revealed as a witch. The spirits are good friends, but they can be capricious and mischievous.

Then again, if I'd had such a friend when I lived at home, perhaps my father would not have been able to hurt my mother.

Or perhaps it would have made no difference.

Eight days after I'd come to the cottage, I found the grave.

It was a little ways into the forest, not directly visible when standing outside the cottage itself. But it was a fairly straight walk toward the sunrise. I would not have even known that the mound under the tree had any significance, but for the words clumsily carved into the trunk:

Here lies the one known as Frea.

I wondered if Alcina had wished to say more, or if she had been satisfied with the simple inscription. I wondered if she'd ever learned Frea's True name. I wondered if I would ever learn hers.

The forest grew thickly around the clearing surrounding the cottage, but no trees sprouted near the building. Only grass and small flowers grew there, tiny stars of bright yellow and lavender that peeked between the green stalks.

Over the next few days I cleared the garden as best I could, fashioning stakes from branches that the peas could twine around as they grew, thinning the space between the root vegetables, and discovering even more that I hadn't realized were there at first: onions and garlic, mint and chives. Around the edge of the clearing grew flowers that had burst into bloom in the past day, bright white and yellow daisies and roses of pink and red and white.

"Thank you," I said to the air. "Spirit of Vitality, I am grateful to you for the bounty you have provided."

An angry hiss made me shake my head and rub my ear. "*The Spirit of Vitality failed,*" came the Spirit of Wind's words, angrier and louder than I'd ever heard it, a shout of a whisper.

"Failed to do what?"

A sullen silence was my only answer. I shook my head.

"The Spirit of Vitality is providing me with nourishment. Whatever else it did or didn't do, I have reason to be grateful to it."

A huff, then an empty silence. I gathered a few more vegetables in my skirt and carried them into the cottage.

Chapter 8

The diary entries began to grow sparser, the dates further and further apart. The subjects were less about Alcina's past, and more about the mundane realities they faced: people who came to them for help, the difficulty in finding things to eat over the winter (fortunately they didn't have to worry about staying warm or gathering firewood), the scarcity of certain herbs they used in their concoctions. The entries became shorter as well, but I read each one with the attention and devotion one would give to holy writ, hungrily gathering each crumb of Alcina I could find. All in all, she kept the diary for nearly two years, even if her entries were increasingly sporadic and brief.

Eventually there came a gap of time where she didn't write at all. Indeed, I thought that the diary was finished, for the page was blank, before I turned to the next and found it filled, the date a full half year after the previous entry.

Frea is sick. No, not sick. She is dying. All of her knowledge of herbs and medicines has not helped. And all of my knowledge comes from her.

I disobeyed her. I've never done so before, but I thought, if there are spirits that can make light and heat and warmth, could there not be spirits of healing or strength? I have gathered together what I need for the ritual, and tonight I will perform it after she is asleep.

Many of our medicines restore vitality, but none have restored hers. So I will summon a Spirit of Vitality, to help boost her failing strength and give her back the energy she has lost.

I am sure it will work.
It must work.
I cannot lose her.

The book shook in my hands. It hadn't worked. Or had it? Perhaps for a time?

But no, the Spirit of Wind had said as much. The Spirit of Vitality had failed. It hadn't been able to save her.

I thought of what it would be like to lose Alcina, my dearest friend and companion.

I knew it was different. My feelings for her were not those of a daughter. Frea had been a mother to Alcina, and Alcina had tried to be one to me. But the shape of our relationship was different.

Regardless, Alcina had loved Frea and depended on her. How painful it must have been when she was left alone.

I failed. The Spirit of Vitality cannot help Frea, or so the Spirit of Wind tells me. It tried, but her body is too weak to withstand it.

I will not give up. If not vitality, then endurance. I will summon a Spirit of Endurance that she may be stronger, and then the Spirit of Vitality can help restore her life.

She doesn't even know what I've done — she has been too tired, her mind wandering and confused. I will wait to tell her until she is well.

Oh, *Alcina*, I wanted to cry out. I wanted to wrap my arms around her younger self and press her close, pull her head to my shoulder and comfort her.

I already knew she would fail.

I put off reading the next entry for several days. Instead I went back to the books on herbs, re-reading them and even attempting a few of the simpler recipes. Much of the miscellany on the shelves bracketing the fireplace made sense when one knew what the various recipes called for, though some of it was still a mystery.

The book on summoning spirits was, as I had already determined, not among the books in the cottage. I was certain that Alcina had brought it with her to the castle.

"Spirit of Wind," I asked cautiously, "is the Spirit of Endurance still here?"

"*Yess,*" the Spirit of Wind replied. I was prepared for it this time, but still flinched a little at the hiss. "*It makes the walls ssstrong,*" it said, a note of mockery in its tone. I reached out and placed a hand flat on the whitewashed stone as though I could feel it, but it felt like a wall, nothing more. Not like the active Spirit of Wind or Spirit of Warmth. Still, the Spirit of Endurance must permeate the walls, the floor, even the roof of the small building. No wonder the house had not suffered from deterioration, despite how long it had been left alone.

"Spirit of Wind," I said again. "When Alcina left... were you lonely?"

A tickle along my arms. "*What is... lonely?*"

I opened my mouth, then closed it again. "Never mind," I said at last, and let my hand drop away from the wall.

Eventually I could delay no longer. Settling onto the bed, I requested more light, which the Spirit of Light graciously provided, and began to read.

The Spirit of Endurance cannot help her.

Every day she weakens further. She has told me that the cottage is mine, and all that is in it. What do I care for the cottage, for the books and the supplies, if she leaves me alone? I will have only the Spirits left for company.

I will try one last time. A Spirit of Perseverance, that she may survive this. If this fails, I —

The sentence ended in a smear of ink.

Unable to stop, I turned the page. The following page was blank except for three words, the writing unsteady and blurred but still legible:

I have failed.

I paused there, staring down at the stark, unhappy truth. Alcina. My darling Alcina. My own heart twisted with shared grief, for Alcina's sorrow and loss, and for the fact that I would never meet the woman who had been so dear and so important to my beloved.

Wiping my eyes, I turned the page. The date was a week later from the previous entry.

I have been discussing matters with the Spirits I conjured, the Spirit of Wind helping us communicate. Poor Wind is angry that they couldn't save Frea, which I'm afraid is my fault. I should not have raised Wind's hopes, nor my own. Reading further into the book on True Magic, I have come to understand what I should have grasped far sooner, and would have, if I'd been clearer headed. Spirits cannot affect humans, not in the way I'd hoped. They can alter the environment, but living creatures are too complex.

I should have guessed. After all, if there was such a thing as a Spirit of Healing, Frea would have summoned one years ago, rather than relying on herbs and concoctions when helping people. Or if not Frea, someone else would have.

Perhaps, if I'd focused my efforts on understanding the properties of the herbs and hadn't chased after a false hope, Frea would —

No. I cannot allow myself such thoughts. She asked me to go on, to be strong without her. I will do my best.

Taking a shuddering breath, I closed the diary and set it aside.

"Spirit of Wind," I said, forcing my voice steady, "Is the Spirit of Perseverance here as well?" I knew the answer, and went on before it could reply, "Oh, of course it is. That's why the water has remained fresh, and the food, isn't it?" The grain I'd found in the cupboard, the dried vegetables I'd discovered in the cellar — even the stew I'd made, which had lasted until I'd finished it, days longer than I'd expected it to. There had been none of the rot or mildew I would have expected in a wooden cottage, especially one built in the middle of a forest that received rain on a regular basis.

"The Spirit of Perseverance keeps the food," the Spirit of Wind agreed grudgingly. *"Keeps it fresh and good."*

"It's more a Spirit of Preservation than a Spirit of Perseverance," I murmured, and felt something like a breath of laughter weave through my hair. "A Spirit of — of Keeping."

"It likes that," said the Spirit of Wind. *"It says you may call it that."*

"Does it? Then that is what I shall call it," I declared. "Thank you, Spirit of Keeping."

There was no response, of course, but The Spirit of Wind gave a breathy, bubbling giggle which I took to be a 'you're welcome'.

"Would any of the rest of you like a different name?"

I asked, looking around at the cottage. "Spirit of Wind, of Warmth, of Light—are you happy being called those?"

A touch to my cheek. "*We are happy,*" whispered the Spirit of Wind.

"And you, Spirit of Vitality, Spirit of Endurance, would either of you choose a different name?" I asked, and waited.

After a moment, the Spirit of Wind said, "*What names?*"

Caught unprepared, I stammered, "Well, uh, I could call the Spirit of Vitality something like—like 'The Spirit of Growth' instead?"

Another moment of quiet, presumably while the Wind communicated with the others. "*The Spirit of Growth likes that name.*"

"As for the Spirit of Endurance...I would suggest that you're a Spirit of Durability, or more simply, a Spirit of Strength."

"*The Spirit of Strength prefers that.*" There was another moment, as though of hesitation. "*Names are important.*"

"They are. These names are simple and easier to say. Spirits of Wind, Warmth, Light, Growth, Strength, and Keeping. Thank you, my friends." I tilted my head back and opened my arms, laughing as I felt wind and warmth sweep along them. The light dimmed and brightened again.

When I finally dropped my arms, Wind whispered, "*Names should be true.*"

"Yes," I said, thinking of the name Alcina had chosen for me. 'Snow White', she'd called me. Had it merely been a spur of the moment choice based on my skin, or was there more to it? Had she been thinking of my innocence, my purity?

The Spirit of Endurance hadn't helped Frea endure, the Spirit of Vitality hadn't given her life, and the Spirit of Perseverance hadn't helped her survive. It was no wonder they wanted different names. And I was not "Snow White" anymore, not even in looks—my cheeks were ruddy from hard work and my skin darkening from the time I'd spent in the sun, a flock of freckles making their home on my nose and cheeks.

And the way I felt about Alcina was neither innocent nor pure. I wondered what name she would call me by if she knew the truth.

The Spirits have all chosen to stay. They regret not being able to help, I think, though their words are of course filtered through Wind's bitterness. At least they can understand me, even if they cannot answer. I told them that they are free to leave, or that I can discorporate them if they would prefer, but they all wish to remain.

It is just as well. I have barely been able to feed myself the past weeks, let alone think of anything else. If the Spirit of Perseverance had not kept such food as I had from spoiling, I might well have starved.

For years I slept on a bed of blankets on the floor, but I have finally moved into Frea's bed. It feels strange after so long on the ground, but it doesn't feel as wrong as I'd feared it would. She wanted me to have the cottage and everything in it. She had no children of her own, and was pleased that I would carry on her legacy. I will honor her and continue her work.

The entry ended there. I frowned at the page, glancing at the date. She'd written it only a few months before my father had brought her home with him.

There weren't many pages left in the thin book. Greedily, helplessly, I kept reading.

I have been gifted the most extraordinary thing by a grateful mer-

chant. It is a mirror, nearly as tall as I am, and beautifully framed. I cannot imagine how much it's worth. Yet I have no idea what to do with it. It is useful, I suppose, in helping me improve my disguise. I have been dressing like Frea, pretending I am old when I must leave the cottage, so that people will leave me alone.

I did not like the way the merchant looked at me when he gifted me the mirror. Thankfully my darling Spirit of Wind encouraged him to leave, blowing on the back of his neck until he shivered, convinced that my cottage is haunted! He left precipitously, and Wind chased him into the woods, pushing and tearing and howling at him the whole way!

I had to stop and laugh at that. I could see it vividly, picturing one of the many merchants I'd met who was respectful only because I was a princess, but whose eyes still roved and whose hands no doubt would have as well if he'd thought he could get away with it. The vision of such a man driven away pale and shaking, convinced he was pursued by a ghost, made giggles bubble up uncontrollably in my throat for several minutes before I finally calmed enough to read more.

I will think on what else I can do with this strange treasure. Surely there is something!

I have it!

The words were cramped, yet written with bold, sure strokes, very different from the hesitant writing of the earliest entries.

I will summon one more spirit. I snorted. Alcina, darling, hadn't you learned your lesson yet? None of the other spirits she'd summoned had behaved as she'd hoped. What made her think this one would?

It has been so gloomy without Frea. Of course, the wonderful Spirit of Light keeps the house bright, and Wind helps me keep it free of dust, and the others all contribute as well. But things are all so very much the same from day to day.

I was reading about the different types of spirits, and came across one called a Spirit of Beauty. If I can conjure one and convince it to live in the mirror, perhaps it can show me beautiful things! Vistas of flowers, mountains, even the seaside! I've always wondered what the ocean looks like. It will be like having a lovely painting that changes all the time!

I laughed again, helplessly. "Alcina," I said aloud, and felt the air stir, rustling the pages.

For years my so-called stepmother had seemed reserved and cool, untouchable and proud. She was warmer with me, but even then, she retained a dignity and a distance that I'd dared not try to cross or puncture.

All that time, this sweet woman had been inside her, as eager and impulsive as I'd ever been, and a lot more creative. She'd been...I counted back through the dates...all of nineteen when she'd written this, the same age I was now!

Well, it worked, the next page read, *but not quite the way I hoped it would.*

Of course it hadn't. I shook my head, smiling so widely that my cheeks ached.

The Spirit will show me beautiful things, but mostly it shows me people.

I suppose it makes sense. What frame of reference would a spirit have for such things? Only what humans say or think is beauti-

ful — and that is frequently other humans. It will show me beautiful places, but only places I've already been.

Still, it is nice, in a way, to see other people. Sometimes it even shows a snippet of conversation. Yesterday it showed me a young sailor declaring that his bride was the most beautiful woman in the world.

It makes me feel a little less alone.

All desire to laugh died.

My poor Alcina. I wondered if the mirror showed her people because that was what Alcina had secretly longed to see, even if she hadn't realized it.

The next entry skipped over many more months.

I found a wounded man in the forest today. He'd been carried off by his horse, who had been hurt and was dying, poor creature. I managed to get him as far as the cottage — the man, I mean, not the horse.

He is feverish and delirious. He keeps calling for 'Margareta'. I am doing my best for him, but I do not know if he will survive.

I'd been out gathering herbs. Unfortunately, I wasn't wearing my disguise when I found him. Old Weldon found another book for me, and I stayed in too long, reading it when I should have been working. In the end it was late enough in the day that I could either gather herbs or put on the disguise — there wasn't time for both.

So the man saw my face, and in his more lucid moments he grasped my hand and told me I was beautiful, an angel from heaven. It was most embarrassing.

The entry ended there.

There were only a few pages left of the book. I set it aside and went out to see what I could find for dinner. Thanks to the bounty of the Spirit of Growth, the deer meat I'd preserved (perhaps unnecessarily, given the presence of the Spirit of Keeping), and the success I'd had setting a few traps for smaller animals, I'd already begun stocking the cellar against the winter to come.

I wondered how long it would take Alcina to join me. My father's campaigns almost always stretched for months at a time. Would she be able to get away from the castle and back to the forest? She would have Gregory on her side, and maybe even some of the servants, but the fear my father inspired would be a deterrent to helping her. If he ordered her locked up in the dungeon, would she be able to use her magic to escape?

At first living in the cottage had been a novelty, alone and without anyone telling me what to do or where to go. I was able to practice my sword forms at whatever time of day I wished—in the cool of the morning or the evening when before I'd had to swelter through the heat of the afternoon. There was much to learn and to do: many books to read, food to be gathered, preparations to be made for the eventual coming of winter. There were the spirits to speak to, even if only the Spirit of Wind could reply. It was such a very different life from everything I'd known before that it took time for it to begin to wear on me.

That day, when I wondered how long it would be until Alcina came to me, was the first time I began to get an inkling of how lonely it was going to be to live in the cottage all alone.

Chapter 9

The days passed. I set aside Alcina's diary, leaving the last few pages unread. I had bolted most of it down too quickly, like a child given an unaccustomed treat, before realizing too late that I only had a bite left. I decided to wait to read the rest, saving it. Tucking it behind the other books, I tried to put it out of my mind.

I began to settle into a routine. On sunny days I spent the mornings exploring the forest, collecting the herbs I was learning to recognize as useful, either for cooking or medicinal purposes. When I returned, sweaty and dirty from my exertions, I would bathe and wash my clothes in the chill stream that ran near the cottage. As the afternoons grew warmer, I began napping during the heat of the day while my clothes dried and spending the cooler early evening outside, training with my sword. As summer approached its height, the sun lingered in the sky each day, giving me plenty of light to work by.

Of course, I could have asked the Spirit of Light for help if I'd wanted to train in the coolest part of the night, when the sun had already set. But despite how friendly the spirits had been, a part of me was still wary about doing so. I did have to ask the Spirit of Warmth for help cooking. And the Spirit of Wind had been right; I was far more inclined to ask them to cool the cottage than I was to ask for warmth as the summer's heat grew more oppressive. But mostly I tried not to depend on the spirits too much.

Yet I could not help depending on them for one thing in

particular: companionship.

I found myself talking to them frequently, speaking aloud my thoughts and fears, my wishes and dreams. Only Wind ever answered me in words, though it rarely understood what I was discussing and would invariably try to turn the 'conversation' back to itself, causing us to talk past each other more often than not. But all of them had their own ways of communicating.

When I took down a pot, the stove would begin heating without me having to say a word.

When I expressed delight at finding strawberries growing in the garden, the next day I discovered more of them, and they were larger and sweeter.

The walls remained strong around me, but more than that, things I wore or used or made would last far longer than they should have. The scratchy, poor fabric of the clothing in the dresser, which had become my daily garments except when I was training, should have fallen apart after being worn and washed again and again. Yet it held together, the seams strong and tight even after weeks of wear. They stayed fresh, too, never growing musty even when an unexpected rainstorm blew in and made everything sticky and damp for three days straight until I gave in and asked Wind and Warmth for help.

On rainy days I didn't go into the forest, preferring to stay in the cottage and read. I read a section of one of the history books each day, a chore I'd set myself before I would allow anything more interesting. As a reward for finishing that, I permitted myself to choose from any of the other titles. I read the cookbooks, the books on medicine, even some of Alcina's romances.

I hadn't often read for pleasure when I'd lived in the castle. Even now I found myself growing restive and impatient after a few pages of story.

I awoke one morning to sunlight in my eyes and realized with a shock that I had no idea how long it had been since I arrived.

"I should have kept track," I said aloud.

"*Track?*" Wind tugged at my hair in greeting. "*Track?*" The 'k' sound was a ticklish puff against my ear.

"Of the days since I arrived here," I said, rising and slipping on the simple, homespun clothing I'd left at the foot of my bed. "I don't know how long I've been here."

"*Why?*" Wind said. "*I will make it cool every day for you. Counting them doesn't matter.*"

"Perhaps not, my friend," I said with a small smile.

The thought weighed on me as I went to prepare breakfast. I tried to count back, but could only determine that I'd left in spring, and it was now well into summer.

An abrupt wave of homesickness crashed over me. I'd always wished for freedom, but I'd never grasped what that might mean. I'd never thought that the price of freedom would be to endure loneliness. And even with all the things that Alcina had tried to teach me, I'd never understood what it would be like to have to live without servants, without anyone supporting me, caring for me, helping me. To have to obtain my own food, my own clothing.

The spirits freed me from the onerous necessities of gathering firewood, of making candles, of so many things. I had to work hard, but not nearly as hard as Frea must have had to when she'd come to this place alone so long ago. It was a wonder that she'd survived. Yet again I regretted that I'd never been able to meet her. But if she'd lived, perhaps I wouldn't have been able to meet Alcina, and that opportunity I wouldn't have sacrificed for anything.

I missed Alcina. She'd been my dearest friend and confidant. I'd tried to put her out of my mind, since the alternative was worrying about her constantly. At any moment my father might return and throw her in the dungeon or behead her in a fit of pique. I trusted that Alcina didn't want to die and I knew she was talented and resourceful, but I also knew very well that there were limits to her abilities.

Panic would sometimes rise within me despite my attempts to fight it. She could be trapped or imprisoned, hurting and afraid. She could be dying. She could be *dead*, and I wouldn't even know it.

My promise held me like chains, but the chains were weakening. Fortunately, the height of summer brought a visitor. The sight of Gregory leading his horse down the path through the woods sent terror and hope through me, my heart attempting to leap and sink simultaneously. Breathless, I ran up to him. "Alcina? How is she? Is she all right? Is she coming?"

He sighed and extracted a wax sealed letter, silently handing it over. "She is well. Your father has not yet returned."

Light-headed with relief, I impatiently pulled open the missive and began to read. Seeing her cramped writing almost brought tears to my eyes, but it was a strangely ordinary letter, discussing palace matters and everyday things. I finished the first page and looked up, realizing that I'd left my guest standing. "I'm sorry," I said, "Please, come in and have some water."

He nodded, stepping up to the cottage and caring for his horse first before coming inside. I obtained a wooden cup of water for him, which he drank appreciatively. "You can finish reading," he said with another sigh, gesturing at the linen paper which hadn't left my grip. "She asked me to wait until you could fashion a reply."

"Of course," I said. I put together a plate of food for him, some vegetables I'd gathered from the garden that morning as well as some of the deer meat I'd preserved. He ate as I sat to finish reading the letter from my—from Alcina.

The second page was as mundane as the first. Gradually it dawned on me that she had not specifically addressed the letter to me, nor had she mentioned anything that could be tied to any activities that might be considered unsavory. It was a letter that might have been sent to anyone, but for a few subtle references to conversations we'd had and things only she and I knew.

It was proof she was alive and doing as well as might be expected, but it told me little more than that. I scowled down at the page. I was glad that nothing had gotten worse, but I'd also hoped that, perhaps, she might have said something about joining me? At least visiting me?

"I wish I could go back with you," I said to Gregory, trying not to sound sullen and failing. "I don't like leaving her alone."

"I know," he said, gruff as ever. "I'm sure you miss her."

I had to close my eyes against the sting. "Yes," I admitted. He said nothing more, but handed me the linen pages and ink he'd brought for me to write a reply.

I considered speaking of things like the spirits, but the care with which she'd written made me hesitate. In the end I mentioned that I'd made some friends, including one who was mischievous, one who was warm, one who brightened up any atmosphere... imagining her pained look made me smile.

The rest I filled with the same sort of coded mundanities that she had, discussing the joys and difficulties of living alone. It said too little, but it would have to be enough. I frowned over it, added a few more notes in the margins, and finally surrendered it to my swordmaster. He'd finished his meal and waited, silent and patient while I dithered.

"Please tell her that—that," I stopped, at a loss.

"I'll let her know that you miss her," he said.

"Yes, but also, I..." I had to stop again. "Please tell her to stay safe," I said at last. It was a reiteration of something I'd said multiple times in the letter in different ways, but it was the one thing I most hoped she would take to heart and most feared she would dismiss.

"I will," he said.

After he'd left, the cottage seemed more quiet than ever. The small taste of human interaction had whetted my appetite for it, as when one doesn't realize how hungry they are until they've had that first bite. I went for a long walk and picked up one of Alcina's romance novels when I returned. Tired and heartsick, I let myself escape into the story and ended up staying up long into the night, reading about a ridiculous heroine and her beau.

My craving, for other people in general, and Alcina in particular, did not go away. As the months passed and the weather cooled, it remained a constant ache and irritant beneath my skin, even during happy moments. It didn't help that my days were very much the same, one to the next, with only books and the capricious spirits for company.

Eventually I decided to take matters into my own hands.

There were plenty of different recipes listed in the herbal guides Alcina had left behind, but there was a certain uniformity to them: "For relief of pain", "For increased vitality", "For reduction of nausea", and so on. The vast majority sought to treat the ills of the body. There were a few that claimed to inspire strange dreams. And there was one which stood out, separated from the rest by blank pages, that required more than just careful mixing and preparation. Alcina's notes said that Frea believed that *this* recipe was True Magic, and that

Alcina herself was inclined to agree.

"To dream of one's beloved", said the page title. Drinking the concoction would, or so the instructions claimed, ensure that they had a vivid dream of their beloved the next time they slept. It seemed a pleasant and harmless enough effect, and a chance to try my hand at True Magic.

I'd attempted, with more or less success, to make many of the various mixtures and unguents. However, one of the herbs I needed for this particular one hadn't grown until autumn took full hold. When I finally found it, I gathered many handfuls and brought it back to the cottage to dry, humming to myself all the while. Wind joined me for part of the walk. I'd learned that the spirits could leave the cottage, but the farther they got from it, the more distressed they became. Eventually they would disappear and I would find them back there when I returned. Still, a little company was better than none.

Creating the magical dream-affecting potion wasn't much different from making tea, except that there was a ritual attached to it. I tried making it first without the ritual, and that night I did dream of Alcina, but it was a vague and formless thing, not the realistic experience promised by the instructions.

The ritual portion involved drawing a magical array, with stones and specific items set at various points. There was a chant to be repeated. I wondered if the spirit-summoning magic Alcina had used had been equally complex, or perhaps more so.

I went through the ritual step by careful step, repeating it a few times to make sure I'd gotten it right before finally drinking down the tea. It tasted the same as it had before. I set aside the cup and went to bed, trying not to hope too hard.

Chapter 10

I was in the familiar front room of Alcina's chambers, with its shelf of books and its graceful furniture. For a moment, I could barely breathe, swamped with homesickness and nostalgia. In some ways, this set of rooms held more happy memories for me than did my own.

"Alcina?" I said quietly. There was no answer, so I made my way back to her bedroom, boldly sticking my head through the doorway. "Alcina?"

She was sitting up in her bed, and stared at me as though startled. As I watched, her expression melted into the warm smile she always reserved just for me. "Snow White," she said.

I was nearly overcome with shyness, a malady that had never afflicted me before.

"Alcina," I said, feeling heat rise to my cheeks. I forced myself to take a step forward, then another, reminding myself that it was a dream. "I've missed you."

"As I have you," Alcina said. She was wearing her thinnest nightdress, one of pretty linen and lace. Still smiling, she lifted one hand and gestured. "Come and sit with me. Tell me how you have been."

I obeyed, slipping onto the bed beside her. She gracefully slid over, making room for me, and we leaned up against the headboard, side by side. The bed curtains were sheer and white, softening the glow from the room. It had been a long time since I'd read by candle or lantern light. I wondered if Alcina had missed the clear, bright illumination that the Spirit of Light could provide upon request.

How had I gotten here? I remembered living in the cottage, but when had I left it and returned to the castle? I couldn't remember the ride here. What was the last thing I could remember?

Ah. I was dreaming. I was dreaming, yet I knew I was dreaming. It was a lovely feeling. I felt that I could do anything I wished, could even lift off the ground and fly, but I didn't want to change a thing. Not the sensation of the smooth sheets as I ran my hand along them, the faint smell of wax from the candles, the warmth of Alcina's body next to me. It felt like I was home again.

But it was assuredly a dream. Though we had shared many small intimacies such as helping each other with our hair and clothing and jewelry, we'd never sat together on her bed like this. She'd never allowed me to do anything more than a servant might have done for her.

"This is a dream," I said impulsively.

"I know," she said, calm as always.

A sudden desire spiked through me: to shake that calm for once. I bit my lip, fighting the temptation, but after all, it was only a dream. "Alcina," I said again, and leaned closer.

She went still as I neared her, but did not back away—not even when I tilted my head and brushed my lips against hers in the lightest of kisses.

"Snow White," she whispered, her breath coming out in a rush as though she'd been holding it.

"Dearest," I murmured.

Color came into her cheeks. "I shouldn't," she said. "We shouldn't." I'd always known she would resist me. It didn't surprise me that this fantasy version of her did so.

"Not even in a dream?" I coaxed.

She hesitated. "It's wrong," she whispered at last. "I'm your *stepmother*."

"It's not real," I countered. "And this may be the only place, the only time we can ever do this. Alcina," I said, suddenly desperate, "let me do this. Let me have you."

Her normally cool facade shivered and broke. Tears came to her eyes, a flush to her skin. Slowly, she nodded.

"Thank you," I said against her lips, "my love." She gave a shudder, but not of revulsion. Her hands slid around my waist, clutching at me. She was so beautiful, her skin soft and warm under my hands. I trailed them down her cheeks, following the paths of her tears with the pads of my fingers before leaning in and doing the same with my lips. A strangled little gasp escaped her throat, and she gave another shudder.

Was this what she was like with my father, I wondered? Or did she retain that tight control over herself with him, not letting him have any of her vulnerabilities? I shoved the questions aside. I didn't wish to think of her with her husband, and such questions would do me no good here, with a fantasy version that would probably tell me whatever I most wished to believe.

I remembered the way I had touched myself, how I'd started with my ears and face and neck. Lifting both hands, I slid her hair behind her ears, deliberately sweeping my fingers over and around the curves. Her breath stuttered, sending a lovely little jolt of heat through my core and down to the join of my legs.

She made a jerky motion with her hands, as though she'd wanted to reach out but stopped herself. "You can touch me," I breathed against the top of her ear, following the words with a kiss.

Shaking her head, she gripped the sheets convulsively. "I shouldn't," she said again.

"All right." It would be easier to concentrate on her pleasure without her hands inflaming and distracting me. I kissed her temple, letting my lips linger against her skin. "All right,"

I repeated. I clambered further onto the bed, swinging one leg over both of hers to straddle her. She stared up at me, wide-eyed and blushing. For the first time, I realized how *young* she was. Without her usual armor of heavy dresses and jewelry, she was so much softer. I'd seen her without it before, of course, but never so close. Never like *this*.

"Alcina," I said, cupping her face in my hands, "Do you want this?"

"You *know* I do," she said, sounding almost petulant. "If you are the Snow White of my dreams, you know exactly what I want. Why are you making me say it?"

I felt my lips curve into a satisfied smile. "Because I like hearing you say it." I pressed forward and kissed her on the mouth. She made a small, hungry sound, her hands lifting at last to grab onto my clothing instead of the sheets. I was dressed in a nightdress as well, I noted vaguely, which made sense as things do in dreams. I hadn't worn anything like it since I'd left the castle, but since I was in the castle again, of course I would be wearing it.

Her lips parted under mine. I let myself sink into the kiss. My tongue slipped along her lower lip and dipped into her mouth, shallow and teasing. She gave a start at the first brush of my tongue against hers. Then, hesitantly, she responded.

I'd wanted to touch Alcina for a long time. I'd wanted to feel her touch me for just as long. But somehow it was so much more, even here in a dream. Or perhaps it was *because* it was a dream that it felt like more. Maybe everything was simply more intense: pure lust, pure desire without the difficulties of reality impinging upon us.

Whatever the reason, the movement of Alcina's tongue and lips against mine, timid at first but with growing confidence as she explored, sent such waves of heat through me as I'd never experienced. I finally had to break away, panting, and bury my face in her neck.

"Snow White," she said tenderly, one hand petting my hair and down the back of my head.

"Yes," I said. Desire pulsed between my thighs, where my legs were splayed open around her. I wanted to seize her hand and pull it down between us, but that would be too much, too fast. I wanted to seduce Alcina, not throw myself at her — at least not anymore than I already had.

But that would take time. More than a single night's fantasy. I could perform the ritual again, make more of the magic potion and inspire more dreams, but I already knew I would not. This was wonderful, but it wasn't the truth I wanted. It wasn't the real Alcina, pliant and hot in my arms. The real Alcina would never allow this.

Nevertheless, as long as I was already here...

I would make the most of it. I would enjoy this, my one night with Alcina, even if it was the only one I would ever spend with her and the only way I could ever be with her.

Sitting up, I looked down into her eyes. She had dried her tears, meeting my gaze steadily, the color high in her cheeks and her hair in disarray.

"I want to take off your nightdress," I said. She swallowed and nodded, shifting so that I could tug it out from under my knees and over her head. It didn't catch as it might have if this hadn't been a dream, but slid off smoothly, leaving her bare but for her underclothes. I traced the edge of the soft linen before tugging those off as well, leaving her naked in the muted candlelight.

She was beautiful. Her hips flared a little more than I'd realized, her breasts heavy and soft enough to slide a little to the side. Her nipples were larger and pinker than mine, both beginning to pucker at their abrupt exposure. My mouth watered.

"Are you going to — ah!" Alcina cut herself off with a cry as I leaned down and licked her right nipple, tracing my tongue around the areola in a circle before flicking it across the tightening bud at the tip.

"Am I going to what?" I said against her skin.

"Are—are you—oh—" Apparently she could not finish, at least not when I was sucking on her nipple. Her body shifted under mine, her hips rocking up, and hot satisfaction rolled through me.

When I lifted my head at last, her right nipple had contracted into a tight, flushed peak. Her left was still mostly smooth. That wouldn't do at all.

"Are you going to get undressed?" she gasped out quickly as I lowered my head once more.

I paused, my mouth a half an inch from her skin, my breath stirring across it. "Do you want me to?"

"I—yes!" she said. "I—I want—" Again she interrupted herself, her breath catching as I licked her left nipple. I toyed with it as I had with the other, licking and flicking it by turns before sucking it like the most delightful sweet.

That was a thought. Sticky honey against her skin, where I could lick it off until none remained. Or perhaps the other way—Alcina had a secret love of sweet things, though she did not allow herself to indulge often, perhaps because she knew the difficulties of obtaining honey and syrup in quantity. When such things were offered, though, she would accept them with a quiet delight. Would a little honey dripped over my breasts make her more comfortable putting her mouth on them?

The idle thought was swept away as Alcina tugged at my shoulders. I lifted my head, pleased to see both nipples standing tight and red.

"Take—this—off," Alcina said, pulling at my nightdress. I laughed and sat up, shifting to peel away the linen garment and toss it aside, making the sheer curtains around the bed flutter before drifting down again. Alcina stared up at me, her pupils so wide that the bright blue of her eyes had been reduced to a sliver of color. "So beautiful," she said, then looked away, squeezing her eyes shut.

Heat crawled under my own skin, and I knew my face must have gone as red as a ripe apple. The compliment struck me to the heart. "Th-thank you," I said, suddenly awkward.

That drew her gaze back to me, and she grinned in a way that I'd rarely seen, mischievous and bright. "*Now* you're shy?" she laughed, and reached for my breasts. Instead of putting her mouth on them, she pinched and rolled my nipples between her fingers until I writhed, the throbbing ache between my legs becoming unbearable. In retaliation, or perhaps self-defense, I again reached for her breasts. I lifted them, heavy in my hands, and ran my thumbs over and around the peaks of her nipples, concentrating on the movements of her body beneath mine, the involuntary shivers and jolts and the way she began to arch against me, pressing her breasts into my hands and grinding her hips up against me.

When her hands began to falter, I pulled away and kissed down her body, lingering between her breasts and the soft skin of her stomach, down to the triangular thatch of dark golden hair below. I pressed a kiss in the center of that as well, earning a startled gasp before I let my gaze drift lower. I found the little nub easily, surrounded by flushed skin like the petals of a tiny rose.

"S-Snow White!" Alcina squealed as I leaned in to kiss that tempting target. "W-what— *don't!*"

I froze, then lifted my head. "Why not?"

"It's — it's dirty."

I laughed. "You had a bath not two hours ago," I said. Even if it weren't true, I was certain it would be in my dream. "And this isn't even real."

"But," she shook her head, "but you still shouldn't — "

All desire to laugh faded, and I felt my brows draw to-

gether in a frown. "You read the same books I did," I said.
"You know that this is—"

"Books?" she interrupted.

"The ones on marital relations," I said, growing impatient. "About what two people may do together to give each
other pleasure. Men with women, and men with men, and
women with women."

She stared. "I have read no such books."

"But—" I sat back on my heels. I'd been certain that
she had found and read them as I had. At the very least, I'd
thought that Frea would have given her the volume about
what men and women might do... but no, Frea had died long
before Alcina had met my father, she would have had no reason to give it to her.

I felt a chill at the mere thought of my father. I gave my
head a little shake. "Alcina, did...the King never put his
mouth on you like this?"

"*What?* No, of course not!"

My frown became a scowl. Selfish bastard. Or perhaps
he hadn't known...? "Did he at least—" I cut myself off, not
sure if I wanted to know. Not sure it mattered, since none of
this was real.

Why was my imagination even coming up with this?

A thought struck me, and I felt my heart leap into my
throat. What if, rather than dreaming of one's beloved, the
magic potion made one dream *with* one's beloved? What if
Alcina and I were sharing the dream?

Sense quickly reasserted itself. Alcina would never respond to me as the dream version had.

I took a breath, but before I could speak again, Alcina said
fumblingly, "He—he touched me first, with his fingers, and
then he, he put his—his—"

"Did you enjoy it?" The question spilled out without my
permission, and I read the answer in her eyes even before I

blurted, "I'm sorry, I shouldn't ask —"

"It was uncomfortable," she said, her face twisting with unhappiness. "It — I didn't —"

"Oh, Alcina." I surged forward and pulled her against me. How had my dream become this? Was it that I wanted to be the only one to give Alcina pleasure? Was I that selfish, that my dreamself would come up with such a thing? "Let me make you feel good," I begged. "Please, let me."

Her hand stroked down the back of my head again, as she had done many times. A safe gesture, one that I had yearned for long before I'd known the depth or meaning of my feelings for her. "I can never deny you anything," she sighed.

"I can use my fingers instead," I said, trying not to sound too eager.

I felt her wavering, and her sudden relaxation. "It's a dream," she said. "If you want to — to use your mouth," I lifted my head and met her eyes, wanting to see her expression, "you can," she finished firmly.

Crawling backward once more, I let my fingertips slide down her body, feeling the shape and warmth and softness of her skin. She wriggled and trembled by turns until I got to where her legs were parted for me. Softly, I stroked over that furled flower, sliding the petals up and down as I liked to touch myself rather than going straight for the center.

The sound she made would surely haunt my dreams for years to come, even ones that weren't magically-induced. Her hips jerked up, then away, then pressed up again. "Do it," she said, her normally even voice strained. "Put your mouth on me."

I did.

"Ah," she breathed, "*ah* —" I licked her, tasting salt. No 'nectar' here, but something savory, closer to butter than honey, and more salty and sour than sweet. That was fine. Alcina might like sweet things the best, but I'd always favored salty and sour flavors.

I licked her again, delighting in the way her body opened to me, her knees turning outward even farther, until they were nearly flat on the bed. Stroking the inside of her thighs, I began to tease.

Gradually, I let myself sink into a thoughtful state, tracing patterns with my tongue: letters and numbers, shapes and spirals. It wasn't so different from practicing sword forms, repetitive but not particularly challenging at first. To my dismay, despite it being a dream, my lips began to numb, my tongue grew sore, and my jaw started to ache. But at the same time, Alcina's responses became more and more pronounced. The sounds she made sank into me like stones into water, leaving ripples of desire in their wake. Every breath hissed through her teeth, every bitten off gasp, every startled cry that she tried and failed to hold back—each one only made me eager for more.

Her body, too, told me what she liked. The fluttering throb against my tongue, the way her hips surged and shifted, the way the skin under my lips grew hot and slick. I drew one of my hands up the inside of her thigh again, to where she was slick and open. Carefully, I slid two fingers inside, the clench of her body around them more gratifying than any praise or success I'd ever known. I pressed them deeper, then pulled them out, and Alcina actually whimpered.

What I wouldn't give to be able to watch her face as I did this, to see her expression twist, her eyes squeeze shut, her mouth fall open as she panted. Perhaps someday I would use my fingers instead so I could—

Ah, no, I wouldn't have this chance again. No matter how real it felt, it wasn't. It would never be real.

Thrusting the thought away once more, I redoubled my efforts and was rewarded by a mewling cry. Alcina's body contracted around my fingers. I didn't stop moving them, plunging them into her as she tightened and released around them, her back arched, her pulse racing under my lips.

Finally, she flailed and reached down to grip at my hair. "No more," she begged, "Ah, Snow White, it's too — it's too —" Obediently, if a little reluctantly, I lifted my head, pressing one last kiss to her quivering, sensitive skin before pulling away and drawing my fingers out of her body.

I moved up the bed to flop beside her, gazing at her face as I shoved my still-slick hand down between my own legs. Her eyes were closed, hints of tears at their corners. As I began to touch myself, they slid open, vague for a moment, then flying wide as she saw what I was doing.

"Let me," she said, rolling over to face me. "Let *me*, Snow White." She reached out and caught my wrist, tangling her fingers with mine for a moment before pushing past them to explore. I shuddered hard as she stroked me, shocks of pleasure shooting deep into my core.

"Alcina," I moaned. "Please."

"*Yes*," she said, greedy as I'd never seen her. "I let you have me, now give yourself to me in turn."

"Yours," I choked out. "I'm yours forever, no matter what. Ah, darling," the wave rose to a crest, faster than I wanted. I'd wanted this for so long, and now my body responded like tinder that had been waiting for a spark. Rocking helplessly into her touch, my lips parted. "Yours, always, always, *Alcina* —" The words caught in my throat. My body clenched hard, pleasure gripping me and shaking me for an endless moment that was still over far too quickly.

Alcina's fingers stilled. Slowly, she drew them away, her eyes never leaving my face. My overstimulated body still jumped and twitched, making me squirm.

"All right?" Alcina whispered.

I gave her a tired smile. "Wonderful," I said. Catching her sticky hand in mine, I tugged it to my lips, kissing her knuckles one by one. Lassitude began to steal over me, my tightly-wound muscles finally relaxing. I sank into the bed with a sigh, still gazing at Alcina.

"Is this really a dream?" she said.

Sighing, I nodded. "It's a dream." I managed a grin. "Want me to pinch you to prove it?"

"Certainly not," she huffed, a pale echo of her normally cool attitude. But I wasn't fooled any longer. Beneath the ice she wrapped herself in there was *fire*.

At least, in my dreams.

I closed my eyes. "It's a dream," I murmured again, not letting go of her hand. "I wish it were real. Oh, Alcina. I wish…" My body felt so heavy. I stroked a thumb over her knuckles and sank into the darkness of sleep.

Chapter 11

Bright sunlight stabbed at my watering eyes. "Light," I called, my voice still rough with sleep, "Can you make it less bright, please? Like when the sun is behind thick clouds." Obligingly, the light changed, fading and turning cool and gray. "Thank you."

As I stirred I became aware of the stickiness between my legs. I rubbed my thighs together beneath the coarse sheet. I was more certain than ever that I could never drink the potion again. The instructions for its creation had warned that it could be dangerous. I hadn't understood—how could a dream pose a danger?—but with the memory of last night still vivid in my mind and echoing through my body, I knew exactly why I didn't dare repeat the experience.

It was *too* good. Alcina had desired me, had let me touch her, had *wanted* me to touch her. The pleasant memory was edged with an aching, formless bitterness. It wasn't real, but I wanted it to be.

It would be so easy to make the potion again. To gather more and more of the rare herbs and make as much as I could. To drink it every night and live more in the dreamworld than the waking. A world where Alcina wanted me. A world where Alcina loved me.

I took a long, shuddering breath. The temptation crept up the back of my neck. I itched to gather more herbs, to make more potion, to jump straight into another dream of Alcina. Perhaps one which would begin with us sitting together as we had so often, she bent over a book or ledger, I over my studies...

Shaking my head, I got out of bed and stripped off the sheet. It needed washing, and so did I.

The days plodded on. The leaves began to turn, the sun rising a little later each day. I successfully resisted the urge to make more of the potion, instead devoting myself to cooking as many different recipes as I could manage with the limited ingredients available to me. Gregory visited once more, bringing another missive from Alcina that said nothing of any importance, yet comforted me anyway. He again waited while I wrote a response. This time I served him the latest recipe I'd made: A rich casserole of carrots, potatoes, and other vegetables from the garden mixed with the deer meat, seasoned with a combination of ground up parsley and salt. It would have been better with bread. I often felt the lack of milk, butter, or eggs when I was cooking, but I was proud of this recipe, especially when he took a bite and made a startled and approving expression that I usually only earned after a great deal of successful swordwork.

Counterbalancing that, at my request we sparred together before he left. He scolded me for neglecting my practice, and I hung my head guiltily. In the heat of summer I'd maintained my practice, but as fall had begun to edge toward winter and the sun to set earlier, I'd started skipping a day here and there. Too often. "I'll do better," I said, and he nodded.

"Good." He handed me a few more things. "She wanted you to have these as well." I frowned down at the first item, turning it over in my hands. It was a blank journal like hers, though with better quality paper and finely bound. The rest was writing supplies. "She thought you might wish to write down your thoughts," he said. I smiled and nodded, fond and sad.

Hopefully Alcina would join me soon. It had been months already. My twentieth birthday was in sight. It wouldn't be long before I would be older than she'd been when she'd met me. "Please thank her for me," I said. "I hope to see her sooner rather than later."

He nodded and led his horse into the dense woods. I watched them go until I could no longer see them through the trees.

I turned the blank book over in my hands a few times, thinking about what I would write in it. What I would tell her, if I could. Should I assume that she would read it, or that she would not? I had read hers, after all.

That reminded me: I'd never finished reading Alcina's experiences, saving the last bit for another day. Perhaps it was time that I finally finish it.

I went back inside. The Spirit of Warmth kept it at a comfortable temperature, despite the creeping chill outside. The pines still wore their dark green needles proudly, but the forest seemed darker without the brighter green of the rest of the leaves. The gray, oppressive sky sat over the world like a great bowl, keeping the air both cool and dense. It was a relief to return to the cottage, where I could request sunshine from the Spirit of Light, and a gentle breeze from the Spirit of Wind. They all liked the attention, and transforming the interior from autumn to spring made my heart lift a little.

I tucked away the journal and writing implements for later, then delved through the books until I remembered where I'd hidden Alcina's journal. Settling onto the bed, I turned to the last few pages and began to read. Only once I did so did I realize why I'd stopped for so long.

I didn't want to read about my father.

The man I saved is slowly recovering. He managed a full bowl of vegetable broth today, and looked at me with eyes that seemed more lucid. But then he claimed to be the king, so I knew he was still confused. It has only been two days. I'm sure he will improve given time.

My lips twisted into a bitter smile. Of course she hadn't believed him. What an outrageous claim, that a man she'd found dying was actually the king! I wondered how long she'd remained ignorant of his true status.

The next entry gave me the answer.

It turns out I was the one who was mistaken. A messenger showed up at my door today, demanding to see my patient. When I tried to explain that he had been badly hurt and was still recovering, he pushed his way inside anyway. To my astonishment, he went to one knee at the rescued man's bedside and called him, "Your Majesty."

My patient — the king — spoke quietly with the messenger, who then rose, bowed to me, and left.

"You truly are the king?" I asked, and he gave me a bemused smile.

"I truly am," he said. "You did not know? You didn't contradict me."

"No, I was humoring you." I swallowed hard. There was no doubt he knew I was a witch. Perhaps, in gratitude for my help, he would spare my life.

He laughed at my words. "Usually when people humor me, it's because they are afraid, not because they think I am mad."

"I merely thought you confused," I said quickly. "I was certain you would recover in time."

"Clearly I have," he said, pushing himself into a sitting position. "For I remember exactly who I am." I hurried forward to help prop him up, a protest dying on my tongue. I didn't dare scold him for trying to rise before he was ready.

117

He caught my hand, wrapping both of his around it. "You saved me," he said.

My heart was beating so fast, like a tiny bird's wings in my chest. "I only did my duty."

"You didn't know who I was," he countered.

"It is my duty to help those in need," I told him. Perhaps he would leave me alone after all.

His next words dashed that kindling hope. "Return with me."

"Return?"

"Come back to my palace with me. You are the most beautiful woman in the land. I would like you to be my bride."

My heart froze in my chest.

What could I say? If I denied him, would he have me tried as a witch?

But if I married him, would he tire of me as my father had my mother? Would he kill me?

I asked for a little time to think on it, and he squeezed my hand and said that I had a day.

I ache to have Frea back, to speak for me or at least advise me. I wish I had worn my disguise, even though I know I would never have kept it on once I returned home with the wounded king.

What should I do?

The entry ended there. I felt my brow furrow. I knew the decision she would make. The decision that was no real decision at all, for how could one deny the king?

I turned the page.

I have decided.

Living in the woods I have been sheltered and shielded from the truth, but I am not completely ignorant of the state of the kingdom. Too many have come to us with poorly-healed severed limbs and other grievous wounds. Too many we were unable to save.

I know how those wounds were acquired. I know how the land

and the people have suffered under the king, how he is grinding it into the ground with his ceaseless wars, one after the other.

The king is pleased with me. He says I am beautiful. He wishes to marry me.

These feelings will surely not endure, but perhaps, while I have influence over him, perhaps I can sway him. Perhaps I can keep him at the castle, rather than off waging war. I do not know if I can inspire in him the depth of devotion to draw him away from his love of battle for good. But even a respite, even a year or two of peace would help restore the land and the people.

As for my own feelings, do they matter? Do I not have a duty to do this?

And in truth, is there any alternative? I could flee, perhaps. I could make my way into the woods, or try to cross the border and begin a new life. But if men are not used to being thwarted, surely kings are even less so. Wouldn't he be furious at my rejection? Would he have me hunted down and killed?

Today I will tell him that I accept his proposal.

I pressed my lips together. I didn't know the answer to her questions, but it didn't matter.

I turned the page.

This will be the final entry I will make in this journal.

The king was pleased. He has arranged for men to come and carry my things away. I will bring the books that reference True Magic, and a few supplies, and I have asked to bring the mirror. The king laughed at that, saying that all women are vain, even those who live in the middle of the woods.

I did not enlighten him.

Perhaps it is foolish to bring the mirror. It is large and difficult to transport, and even swathed in cloth will doubtless draw attention and complaints from those tasked to bear it. But if I can take even one of my dear spirits with me, I will not feel quite so alone.

The others are all bound to this cottage and the surrounding land. The Spirit of Beauty is the only one that can accompany me. It may be useful as well. Yesterday I whispered to it to show me the one who the king thinks is the most beautiful in all the land and was shown an image of myself. Someday the king's eye will stray to another. It is best to be prepared when it happens. Perhaps with a little advance knowledge I can save myself and not meet the same fate as my poor mother.

I sighed and turned the page, expecting it to be blank, but found a final postscript, one that looked to be hastily-written:

It turns out the king has a daughter, one not much younger than myself. He has told me that I will be taking her in hand and caring for her.

This will require further thought. I will ask him more about her on the way.

Now I must secretly bid the spirits farewell. I hope they will not be as lonely without me as I will be without them.

My eyes stung. I wiped them and carefully leafed through the last few pages, but they were blank.

I missed Alcina. I missed my life as a princess, with all of its privileges and restrictions. I missed so many things, but I also knew that I would miss this simple life if I should ever have to leave it. The thought of leaving behind the spirits and returning to the castle sent a pang through my heart. How much worse must it have been for Alcina, the same age as I was now, leaving behind the closest thing she had to family and being taken to a place she knew nothing of to marry a man she felt nothing for?

I wished I could go back in time and somehow change things. But would I if I could? Would I change things so that we never would have met? I wasn't sure I could give that up.

It didn't matter. No magic was strong enough to change what had already occurred. We could only move forward together, each of us trying to protect the other and hoping that we would survive.

Chapter 12

The first snowfall came late in the year. The days had grown very short, the sun rising late and sinking early, the wind becoming frigid and unpleasant. I spent more time inside, and was deeply grateful to the spirits that cared for me and helped me.

I slept late those days. There was little point in rising before the sun, when the land was so dark and cold. I'd stored a fair amount of food (thanks in part to the help of the Spirit of Keeping) and had no need of firewood, so there was little to do but read the books Alcina had left behind.

I wanted to see Alcina with a deep ache that was nearly physical. So great was the temptation that eventually I was forced to discard the rarest and most critical herb used in the dream spell. It was probably a waste, but when I tossed it into the icy but still-flowing stream and watched it float away, I felt as though a weight had been lifted from my shoulders.

As it turned out, it didn't matter. I saw Alcina in my dreams anyway—not the vivid, crystalline, too-real version induced by the spell, but flickering and warm impressions of her, her hands, her lips, her body. With the help of the hidden books, I spent more time exploring my own body, and I did not scold myself for thinking of Alcina as I did so.

I knew what I wanted. I knew I would never have it. But that made it no less true. No less real.

The first snowfall of the year was light, covering the ground with dry, delicate flakes.

The second was three days later, blanketing everything with a heavy layer of white.

Partway through that night came a loud rapping at my door. I blinked and called to the Spirit of Light, requesting illumination, then cautiously answered the summons.

An old woman stood in the doorway. She was hunched over, her nose hooked, her skin wrinkled. She wore a heavy cloak with a hood that shadowed the upper part of her face.

"Please, come in," I said, guiding her inside. "What are you doing out here, granny? You must be half-frozen!"

She stepped lightly inside and pulled back her hood. Her hair was grey, tied back from her face with a dirty string. She glanced around, then met my gaze.

Her eyes were the brightest blue I'd ever seen.

Gasping, I darted forward. "Alcina?"

She smiled at me, folding her face into many creases and revealing a mouth of missing and half-rotted teeth. When she spoke, though, her words were perfectly clear. And her voice was the same beloved one I had heard a thousand times.

"Snow White," she said, and hope boiled up within me, then died down again at her next words. "We don't have much time." I reached for her hand. It was soft and cold in mine, not the wrinkled and bony appendage it appeared to be.

"What has happened?" I asked.

"Your father has returned," she said. "He discovered that you were not in the palace. At first he threatened to kill me if I didn't reveal your whereabouts, but then he remembered the cottage where I'd been living when I found and healed him. He is on his way now. I slipped away, but they will soon notice my absence."

"We must flee—" I began, but she shook her head.

"I have a plan," she said. "Snow White, do you trust me?"

"Of course," I said.

From inside her cloak she drew something as unexpected as the illusion that covered her beauty. It was an apple. At a time when every one of its brethren had surely already fallen and grown soft, it was as red and ripe and perfect as though it had been plucked not an hour before. "I would prefer to use a less dangerous method, but this was all I had at hand."

I accepted the fruit and lifted it to take a bite.

"No!" She grabbed my wrist and shook her head violently, some of her gray hairs coming free and whipping back and forth with the motion. "Listen to me. Don't bite into it yet. Once your father comes here, take a bite of it and hold it under your tongue. Do *not* swallow it."

I stared down at the beautiful apple, confused. I hadn't read about anything like this. It had to be made with True Magic. "What will it do?"

"If you swallow it, it will poison you, and you will die," she said. "But if you hold it under your tongue, it will merely put you to sleep for a time."

"*Asleep?* What good will that do?" I couldn't protect Alcina if I was asleep!

"I don't have time to explain," Alcina said. I could feel the tension in her hand on my wrist. Her gaze was focused and intense. "Promise me that you will do as I ask."

"But—"

"Promise me, Snow White!"

Swallowing hard, I nodded. "I promise."

Her shoulders slumped in relief, more visible than usual on the already-hunched body. "Good. I must return. I will see you soon."

"Alcina," I said, a terrible suspicion creeping into my heart, "Did you make this apple for yourself?"

She looked away. "Yes."

"Alcina!"

"Only if I had to," she whispered. "I only would have swallowed it if I had to."

My teeth clenched. "I want to protect you."

"I know," she said. She squeezed my wrist, then released it. With one last look around the cottage, she said, "Ah, my spirits. I miss you." Her hair stirred in a sudden breeze, making her laugh. "I'm sorry," she said to them and to me. "I must go." And with that, she turned away.

Everything in me screamed not to let her. I clenched my hands into fists to prevent myself from reaching out and clutching at her cloak, pulling her hard against me, and never releasing her again. "Alcina," I said, my voice hoarse, "I don't want you to die."

She stilled, her hand on the door. "I don't want to die," she said. "I will not seek death, I promise you. But I don't know…" She didn't have to finish the thought. She didn't know if we could both be saved. "Do not forget your promise, Snow White," she said, and disappeared into the cold and dark night with a swirl of snow. The muffled crunch of galloping hooves was quickly swallowed by the night.

I waited. Occasionally I would look out the doorway, watching the snow pile higher and higher. Wild and implausible hopes kept flitting through my mind. What if my father foundered in the snow, falling off his horse and breaking his neck? What if he decided I wasn't worth the trouble and gave up to return home instead?

Slowly, the sky lightened, going from black to dark gray to lighter gray. I ate a small meal and said to the spirits, "I may have to leave you soon."

"Leave?" Wind's whisper brushed against my ear. *"Will you return?"*

"I don't know," I said. "I will try to come back if I can."

The breeze died down into an unnatural stillness for a time. I finished the tea I'd made and cleaned and returned the dishes to their places. My thoughts shied from my father, from Alcina, instead coalescing on the cottage itself. It would be fine without me, I told myself. Wind would keep it free of dust and small pests, while the Spirits of Strength and Keeping prevented rot and mold from taking root in the building. I wandered the small space, putting away the book I'd been reading, making sure that Alcina's journal and the books with marital instructions were carefully hidden, and finally making the bed—something I hadn't bothered to do since I'd arrived.

"We don't want you to leave." The puff against my ear was so sudden that I flinched.

"I wish I could stay," I said. "I'm sorry that I cannot."

"Why can you not?" It was amazing how petulant Wind could sound, considering that the spirit's voice never rose above a whisper.

I considered my response. How could I frame it in a way that the spirits would understand?

"I made a promise," I said at last. "It binds me."

"As we are bound to the house?" There was a trace of hesitation in the response, now.

"A little like that. But I am bound to a person. I must try to protect her."

The house went still again. I went to the door, but saw and heard nothing but the snow swirling in the rising wind. Going to the dresser, I changed out of the coarse, borrowed clothing into the sword training clothes I'd been wearing when I arrived. The fine fabric felt strange against my skin.

"You can be bound to a person?"

"People can," I said. "I don't know about spirits."

A tiny gust of wind stirred my hair. "*Return soon.*" The tone was both imperious and pleading. I wondered again if the spirits would be lonely without us, or if they would forget us. After all, they hadn't known the difference between Alcina and myself at first—though Wind had seemed to recognize her earlier despite her disguise and despite the fact that I still wore the token she'd given to me.

"I'll try," I said.

The cottage shook as someone pounded on the wooden door. I concealed the small apple in one hand and went to answer it.

The gray light was the same inside and outside the cottage, but the huge man standing in the doorway seemed to cast a shadow anyway. It took me a moment to realize that it was my father, decked in full armor but for his helmet, his hand on the hilt of his sword. I backed away from him, sudden fear clutching my throat.

His expression softened slightly as he met my eyes. "Margareta," he said, his tone relieved.

For a moment, I dared to hope that his relief was due to finding his missing daughter. That *I* was the one he was seeing. "Father," I said.

His brow creased. "Do not call me that," he said.

Hearing those words, I knew it would be hopeless. My fingers tightened around the apple.

I didn't want to bite into it. I didn't want to leave Alcina alone and unprotected.

I had promised.

Lifting the apple to my lips, I took a small bite. It was sweet and crisp, the most delicious apple I'd ever tasted. Careful not to swallow, instead I slipped the fragment beneath my tongue as Alcina had instructed.

The world began to fade at the edges, then darken. I felt myself swaying.

"Margareta!" My father's shout hurt my ears, but I couldn't say anything. My knees folded and my body crumpled. Strong arms caught and lifted me. The apple slid from my hand and rolled away, beneath the bed by the sound of it. "Margareta!" my father cried again. Then, "Bring the witch!" he snarled.

I felt my body being laid across my bed. No, not my bed, I thought. Alcina's bed. I'd only been borrowing it.

The sound of heavy boots tramped into the cottage. I could hear someone with a lighter step stumble forward. "Your majesty," came Alcina's beloved voice. I wanted to scream, but could only lie there, still and quiet. This wasn't sleep. This was paralysis of a sort. I was aware of everything, but could move almost nothing: only my tongue, a little, and my jaw, to clench it.

"Is this your doing, witch?" came my father's harsh voice.

I felt gentle fingers brush my hair away from my forehead, then press against my lips. I wanted to kiss them. To clutch them and never let them go.

"She has been cursed," Alcina said. "Only a kiss of true love can awaken her now."

"*True love?*" my father scoffed.

"True love," Alcina said coldly.

"That is simple enough," my father said. I felt something grasp the front of my dress, lifting my limp body. My father's lips pressed to mine.

This was no innocent kiss between parent and child. My father kissed me with a hungry desperation. Fortunately, the control I had over my tongue and jaw was enough that I could bar him entry. Disgust bubbled through my mind, but did not echo in my body. I wished it would. I wished I could spit in his face.

I was lowered gently back onto the bed. "Why is she not awakening?" The desperate rage in my father's voice was terrifying.

"You are not her true love," Alcina said, colder than the winter morning.

"*Who is?*" my father demanded.

I wanted to tremble. I wanted to laugh. If he knew...

"Prince Karl," Alcina said.

What?

If I could have blinked, I would have. Prince Karl was certainly not my true love. Alcina must know that much.

The shape of her plan became clear to me at last, and I spewed silent curses, terrible ones I had learned from the servants, in the privacy of my own mind.

"Prince Karl?" My father's voice was rich with mockery and disbelief. "She has never met the boy."

"She has. The palace guard will confirm it."

"You *dared*—" My father's fury seemed to fill the room. Alcina gave a cry of pain, and I strained to move.

A crash shook the room.

"*You will not harm her.*" The Spirit of Wind had always whispered as long as I had known it, but now it moaned with the sound of a tempest lashing against the walls. I soundlessly cheered it on.

"Wind, no!" Alcina said. "Do not!" I wished I could groan. *Let Wind do as it will!* I wanted to cry. *Let it protect you, when I cannot!*

The unnatural gale began to die down. When it was quiet again, my father gave a short, high-pitched laugh. "Very well, witch," he said hollowly. "We will return to the castle and see if Prince Karl can awaken my wife."

"Yes, your majesty," Alcina said.

I felt myself lifted again, though I still had no more control than a sack of wheat. The weight of my sword at my side was a small comfort to me, even if I could not wield it.

I was settled on a horse, my legs lashed to the saddle and my torso bound to my father's. My head lolled forward, and my father tenderly wrapped a scarf around my chest and the top of my head, keeping it still without choking me.

It was nothing like when I had ridden with my swordmaster.

Once when I was very young, my father had taken me up on his horse before him. The creature had seemed a veritable giant. I remembered his strong arm around my waist as I clutched the reins in my small hands, delighted at being up so high.

It was nothing like that, either.

My heart wept. My father's obsession with battle was bad enough, but this latest delusion hurt more. Though he had been gone for most of my childhood, I had looked up to him for many years, a great and untouchable figure that the servants had spoken of with reverence.

It was only when my stepmother had begun to show me the truth that I had lost my awe of him and come to understand that, although he had once been a good man and a good ruler, he was no longer either.

In a sense he'd been right. I didn't believe that Alcina had bewitched me. I knew her too well to believe it. But she was nevertheless the reason that I had 'turned against' him. If I had not known her and he had still come to the same absurd conclusion, what would I have done? I couldn't believe that I would have allowed him to marry me, to touch me. But in a palace without allies, how could I have escaped? Would I have fled? Would I have taken my own life, rather than bend to his will?

Such dark thoughts swirled through my mind as the snow gusted around us, stinging my cheeks. My father had wrapped me in an extra blanket, but I was tossed around on the saddle despite his care. I could feel it all, but could do nothing about it.

At last the muffled thump of horse hooves changed as they struck stone. We were arriving at the streets of a town, then, one that had swept the cobblestones clear of snow. My father called a halt and ordered his men to obtain a carriage and hot food. The sounds of voices and more hooves filled my ears as they hurried to obey. I struggled to move, even just a finger, but my body remained outside my control.

At last I heard the sound of wheels. The rope around my legs was loosened, and I was carefully lifted down from the back of the horse. I was laid onto the cushions of the carriage, out of the gusting snow.

"The witch will ride inside as well," my father snapped, his voice slightly muffled. "I will not have my people staring at her and my future wife. You and you, ride with them. Make sure that the witch doesn't try anything."

Alcina would be inside with me! If only I could speak to her, could beg her to kiss me and awaken me!

I was leaned against something soft and yielding. A scent of cinnamon and cloves came to my nose and I tried to breathe more deeply, but I could not do even that.

"Bear with it a little longer, Snow White," Alcina whispered.

"Do not speak to her," came the voice of one of the men. The carriage began to sway, pressing me into Alcina's side more firmly.

We traveled in silence, the sound of horse's hooves loud and then muffled again as we left the town and made our way toward the capital.

"Does the king truly intend to wed the princess?" the second of the two men asked.

"It is nothing to us what he chooses to do," the other said sharply.

"But—"

"Mind your orders," said the first man. "Anything else is not your concern."

"It's wrong," mumbled the second man.

"Whatever the king does is right," said the first, but I could hear a desperate exhaustion beneath his tone. Perhaps he had to believe his own words, after seeing so many battles.

There was a mutinous silence from the second man, and I blessed him in my mind, wishing I could reward him in some way. If I made it out of this alive, I would ask Alcina if she knew his name.

The rest of the trip was uncomfortable, but not painful. I was warm enough in the layers of blankets, and happy to be with my beloved. I continued to struggle against the magic, testing its limits.

I tried to open my eyes again, and this time I managed to crack them open the slightest amount. I could see little, unable to turn or lift my head, but I could make out the edges of the men's boots. Beneath my mostly-closed eyelids I shifted my gaze to the side, where I could barely make out the edges of Alcina's clasped hands. They were bound before her, sitting loosely in her lap.

How *dare* he bind her.

Until now the anger at my father had been formless and vague. I'd been frustrated and furious that he'd ground down our country into a shadow of its former self with his unnecessary wars. I'd been disgusted and hurt when he'd kissed me. I'd been afraid when I saw him declaring that I was his wife, and when I'd seen him outlined in the door of the cottage.

But the sight of Alcina's delicate wrists bound and chafed

by coarse rope sparked such wrath as I'd never before felt.

I wanted to kill him.

Though the trip seemed endless, I did not grow hungry or thirsty, nor did my body make any other demands. It was certainly True Magic, to be able to lock my body into such an unchanging state.

I wondered if 'True Love's Kiss' would actually awaken me. I suspected that Alcina had some other plan in mind. Surely she didn't believe that I was in love with Prince Karl? I had met him but briefly, and though we had become tentative friends, I certainly felt no passion for him, nor he for me.

Yet Alcina had wanted me to marry him and bring peace to both kingdoms. If he broke a 'curse' on me with 'True Love's Kiss', it would go far toward reconciling both peoples to our union. It also neatly thwarted my father, who couldn't possibly marry me if I was already married to my savior.

But what of Alcina's fate in that case? Would my father simply stand aside and allow me to marry the prince? Wouldn't he take his revenge upon Alcina for interfering with his plans?

My thoughts darted and spun, filled with disquiet. I wished I could speak. I wished I could *move*.

"Bring them both inside," I heard my father order as the carriage drew to a halt at last. "Confine the queen to her rooms and take the princess to her own. I will take supper first and then bathe."

I didn't like his tone. There was something confident in it, almost smug.

"I will be sending a secret message," his voice came again,

far quietr and muffled by the side of the carriage. "Come to my study after I've eaten."

"Yes, your majesty," came the crisp reply.

I was carried inside. The smell of the castle, grown unfamiliar after so long away, tickled at my nose. Grease and smoke, the harsh smell of lye and the mustiness of the tapestries covering the walls.

My own room was a little better, but I sorely missed Alcina's cinnamon scent. I imagined myself burying my face in her throat and simply breathing in, imagined her soft arms tightening around me—

No. Now was not the time for such dreams.

I did not grow hungry or thirsty, nor did I sleep, though of course I appeared to. I felt sensations—cold, heat, discomfort—but not pain. I wondered if the bruises I must have inadvertently collected during the trip would make themselves known when I was 'awakened' at last, or whether the magic would somehow prevent or cure them.

For now I could do nothing but lie where I'd been placed: my own bed, my hands folded across my midsection as though I were dead in truth and my head carefully centered on my pillow. I was able to slit my eyes open again, but there was nothing to see. The room was shadowed and dark, the faint glimmer of the banked fire coming from one side. Across from my bed I could see the top of the tapestry I'd liked growing up, an image of two armored people crossing swords. One of the two was slighter than the other, and I'd used to imagine that it was a woman in armor.

I could barely make out the outlines in the dim room, my vision blurred by my lashes, but my memory filled in the colors and the shapes.

I wished I could sigh, but even that was impossible. Letting my eyes sink fully closed again, I allowed my mind to drift.

Chapter 13

I do not know how long I existed in that half-aware state. Occasionally I forced my eyelids up the tiny amount I could manage and surveyed what little I could see. The quality of the light changed, slowly brightening until the colors of the tapestry were visible.

My door remained closed. I could hear sounds, faint and muffled by the thick stone walls. The ordinary rhythms of the castle wrapped around me, comforting me and soothing my fears. The scrape of metal on stone, the swish of a broom, the busy movement of feet to and fro. My chest rose and fell steadily as I waited.

It was slightly chilly, but I could do nothing about it, not even shiver. I'd been living with the Spirit of Warmth for too long, I told myself, and it had made me soft.

The day went on. No one entered to build a fire or lay a blanket over me. I was certain that Alcina would have if she'd been free to do so. Hope lay heavy in my breast. If only she was still alive, I could bear anything else. Perhaps I could strike a bargain with my father. Perhaps he would let Alcina escape and live in the cottage if I agreed to do as he wished.

Revulsion welled in me at the thought. Yet if it was the only way...

No. If it was the only way, that would mean Alcina and I were completely in his power. He would have her killed regardless.

Why had she come up with such a reckless plan, one which left me helpless to intervene?

The answer was obvious when I considered it. It was specifically so that I wouldn't have a chance to intervene. She
intended for me to marry Prince Karl and end the wars. By
announcing to all and sundry that only a kiss of True Love
could awaken me, she had forced all of our hands. My father
had no choice but to bring Prince Karl to awaken me, and if
the prince could do so, what could my father do but accept
the inevitable?

What could any of us do?

He could have Alcina killed at that point, but the story
would already have spread far and wide: a curse broken by
a kiss of True Love, two war-weary kingdoms united at last,
and a happily ever after for the prince and princess involved.

I wanted to bury my face in my pillow and scream.

Alcina must have sent Prince Karl a secret message, probably by way of my swordmaster. If he removed the sliver of
apple from under my tongue, would I awaken? The prince
could hardly refuse — well, he could, but he desired peace as
much as Alcina did. Perhaps more. He would gladly sell himself to secure a peaceful future.

Was I the only one of the three of us who wanted to find
a different way? Perhaps I was too naive. Perhaps there was
no other way.

The light turned a pale gold as I lay there, lost in my
thoughts. Eventually it became gray and began to fade. The
sun had set.

It wasn't until the room was dark and shadowed once
more that something changed at last. I heard the door swing
open and a man's heavy tread. When he approached the bed,
I realized it was my father.

Cold terror stabbed at my heart. What if he'd decided that
I didn't need to be awake for what he wished from me? It
seemed no more bizarre than his declaration that he would
marry me.

To my relief, he merely slid his arms under my shoulders and knees, lifting me carefully. My sword swung awkwardly, but he ignored it, hefting my body to lay my head against his shoulder and turning to the door.

The castle was quiet. It must have been later than I realized. There was no sound or movement around us, just the flickering of torches along the walls as he carried me, slow but steady, down the long, dark staircase to the bowels of the castle.

To my relief we didn't end up in the dungeons. Instead he brought me to a side room I wasn't familiar with. It felt like a long, wide space. Glimpses of it showed me a long table pushed up against one wall with something on it — a map?

"Clear it away," snapped my father, startling me.

"Yes, your majesty." I couldn't see the man's face, but I recognized his voice. He was one of my father's most trusted generals.

The items on the table were swept aside. I didn't see what he did with them, but in moments I was laid on the bare wooden surface. The ceiling was dark with soot. I wondered how many candlelit strategy meetings my father had held here in this underground room I hadn't even known existed.

"Bring the witch," my father grunted.

"Yes, your majesty," his general repeated. I heard the door swing open and closed again. Was Alcina down here, perhaps locked up in one of the dungeons? I imagined her, humiliated, starved, chilled to the bone. My rage, which had begun to be overtaken by fear, flared up again, burning hot in my chest.

"Don't worry, Margareta," said my father, laying a cold hand to my cheek. "I will free you soon." I wanted to bite his fingers off.

The door opened. The clank of chains came to my ears, stoking my fury even higher. If only I could turn my head and see for myself that Alcina was all right.

"Sit there," ordered the king.

Alcina didn't answer him, but I felt it as she moved across the room. All at once she stepped into my field of vision, then disappeared again as she settled into a chair placed against the wall.

My eyes were still blurred, my lashes blocking much of what I could see. Her face had been little more than a pale oval in the dim room. Still, relief sang through me. She was alive and moving under her own power.

I *would* protect her, come what may. I could not allow my father to kill her.

The door swung open again. "Your majesty, your... visitor has arrived," came the voice of the general once more.

"Bring him in."

A quiet step, and the sound of the door closing. I strained my ears and was rewarded when I heard a catch of breath.

"What is the meaning of this?" Prince Karl's voice was not loud, but it commanded attention.

It was only then that I realized the truth. My father had no intention of making public the fact of my curse or my 'rescue' from it. He must have sent for Prince Karl secretly, and for some reason the prince had agreed.

Probably because he'd also received a communication from Alcina.

I wanted to groan.

The prince would 'awaken' me, and then—and then, what? Would my father actually kill him?

"Margareta is under a curse," my father said. "I am told it requires a kiss of True Love to awaken her." His words were hard, but I caught a faint undertone of mockery in them.

Had he realized that this was a trick designed to secure my future and his cooperation?

"I see." To his credit, Prince Karl sounded unfazed. He

stepped forward and leaned over me. His face was blurred and in shadow, but I thought there was a hard resolution to his expression. "Then I will kiss her."

My father moved forward and just behind the prince. I saw something flash in the king's hands.

I felt more than heard Prince Karl's whisper as he bent close. "Snow White," he breathed, "let me in."

His lips pressed to mine.

A frozen certainty overtook me. If the prince succeeded in awakening me, the king would kill him. It unfolded clearly before me: the moment my eyes opened, the king would step forward, plunging his blade into the prince's back.

I tightened my jaw and clenched my teeth. Even when the prince's tongue pressed between my lips, I refused to let my teeth part enough to let him in. He pressed harder, then raised his head with a frown. I saw the quick helpless glance he gave my stepmother.

Unfortunately, so did the king.

"I knew it," my father snarled. "You planned this between you." He shoved the prince aside, but thankfully didn't stab him. Instead he pressed the dagger to Alcina's neck. I could tell only that she held very still, though I could imagine her expression of cool defiance. "Awaken Margareta *now*, or you will be begging for death by morning."

I cursed myself. I should have allowed Prince Karl to awaken me. Perhaps I could have stopped the king, perhaps called a warning in time. And even if I couldn't have, even if the Prince had been killed, I would have been able to move. I would have been able to protect Alcina.

My stepmother rose. "Very well," she said. "I will take the curse onto myself."

Confusion spun through me, transforming into elation as Alcina took Prince Karl's place. Neither my father nor Prince Karl spoke, though whether they were shocked by the turn of events or merely watching to see what happened, I did not know, nor did I care.

All I cared about was the fact that Alcina's face was nearing mine. I couldn't hold my breath, couldn't reach for her, could only lie there as she brought her lips to mine.

My mind went blank. Her delicate hand came up with a clank of chains, pressing gently against my cheek. My lips parted to her, opening as I would always open to her. For her.

Her tongue slipped into my mouth, sliding against mine, hot and wonderful.

Deftly, she pushed the fragment of apple out from beneath my tongue. Then, before I could stop her, she drew it into her own mouth.

There was no transition, as when one awakens. There was no stiffness, no grogginess. One moment, I was on my back, immobile. The next I was gasping, reaching for my beloved, even as she collapsed onto me, her head lolling and her body limp. "Alcina!"

Had she swallowed the fragment? I grasped her shoulders, panic welling in my breast.

"No — No! Alcina!" The cry left my throat raw.

"Good." The single syllable made my head snap up, my teeth bared. I met my father's gaze, my own burning with hatred. If Alcina had died because of him —

The slide of his sword was very loud in the long room. "I will finish this," he said. "Her head first —"

I was off the table, my own sword in my hand almost before I knew what had happened. "You will not touch her," I spat.

"Her hold on you will no doubt fade once she is dead," he said, sounding resigned.

I risked a quick glance around the room. The general was gone. There were only the four of us: Alcina, half collapsed on the table behind me, Prince Karl, eyes wide, my father, looking irritably at me as though I was an unruly child, and myself, all that stood between my murderous father and my precious stepmother.

"Stand aside," my father said.

"No." I straightened. He narrowed his eyes and swung at me, not hard enough to hurt me. I stood my ground and knocked his blade aside scornfully.

"Hm." His eyes flared, his lips turning up in a grin that bared his teeth. "You have been busy while I've been gone, Margareta." He came at me again.

"My name," I panted as I swung at him, "is," a clang rang out as our swords met, "Snow," metal squealed on metal as my blade slid against his, "*White!*"

"Hah!" He sounded, of all things, delighted. His sword moved again, this time with far more intent, forcing me to parry and dodge.

I was thankful that I'd been wearing my training clothes when they came to me. My father began to fight in earnest, the sound of our blades crashing together so loud that it hurt my ears. Prince Karl backed away from the two of us, and I saw with relief that he was circling around to place himself in front where Alcina had crumpled.

If she was dead —

No, I had to focus. I breathed and moved, breathed and moved, my blade becoming almost an extension of my own body. My father's expression shifted into one of concentration as well, the two of us dancing around each other, neither one taking the upper hand. He was stronger, faster, and had a longer reach than I. But then, so did my swordmaster. And the king was taking care not to hurt me, while I had no such compunctions. I knew the consequences if I lost: Alcina's life would be forfeit, as would my freedom and my body.

Even so, there came a point where I knew I could not win.

My father had battled for his life for decades. His experience surpassed mine by a thousandfold.

I saw the moment when he decided to stop toying with me. I'd managed to scratch his arm — not even his sword arm. Something changed in his expression. It hardened, fierce and proud and angry, and suddenly I could no longer hold my own. He drove me back, drove me back again, sword flashing, blocking every escape route.

A scream rose in my throat, a shout of frustration, of despair. He was going to win. He was going to win, and Alcina was going to die.

His eyes seemed to glow as they caught the reflected candlelight. His mouth was spread in a wild grin, almost a grimace. "Mine," he said. "You will be mine." The flat of his sword came crashing down on the back of my hand, splitting the skin and bruising it. My blade fell to the ground with a clatter.

From the corner of my eye I saw Prince Karl start forward. I made a sharp gesture at him to stay back. I'd fought both of them, and of this I was certain: he could no more win against my father than I could.

"Father," I said, tears stinging my eyes. "Please. Don't do this."

His smile softened, becoming tender. "Don't worry, Margareta. Soon you'll be free of her."

"*Don't worry,*" echoed another voice, a whisper against my ear. "*Be ready.*"

I felt my eyes go wide, then quickly dashed away my tears. Falling to my knees, I let my hand slide to the hilt of my sword. "*Please,* father. Let Alcina go. I'll do anything you wish." It was true enough.

"Margareta, be reasonable," he said, but I was barely listening to his gentle, condescending words. "She has bewitched you — "

"*Now!*" It was a whispered shout against my ear. I seized

my sword and leapt to my feet just as my father's head rocked back as though he'd been punched. He recovered quickly, straightening and bringing his sword up, but it was too late. I swept my sword in a clean arc, slicing open the front of his throat.

His eyes widened, his hand going to his neck. His blood fountained out, spraying the front of my dress and filling the room with its metallic stench. He stumbled and slipped, choking and gurgling as the blood kept spurting out in dark, crimson waves.

He never dropped his sword. Even when he finally went still, even when the blood slowed and stopped at last, his hand stayed tightly gripped around the hilt.

"Congratulations." I looked up to see Prince Karl standing above me, just outside of the sticky pool of red. His face was pale as milk, his voice hoarse. "You've done what my people have been trying and failing to do for years." My own sword slipped from numb fingers, landing with a grotesque splash. I wasn't sure if I'd ever be able to pick it up again.

My gorge rose. I squeezed my eyes closed and clamped my mouth shut, but the smell of iron still filled my nose. I breathed through it as I'd been taught, until I could open my eyes and look down at my father, his body a collapsed husk.

"I killed him," I whispered hollowly. I felt as drained as he was. "I killed the king." My thoughts dragged sluggishly, but a new horror rose like a slow tide. My people... what would they do to me? I imagined myself in my father's place, my head separated more cleanly, my blood staining the ground. I had committed regicide. There was only one punishment for that.

Prince Karl took a step into the pool, the blood rising around and clinging to his boot. He held out his hand to me. "The king is dead," he said, sounding as stunned as I felt. "Long live the queen."

"The queen," I echoed. The words rattled around in my brain, driving out all other thoughts. "The queen. The queen!" I ignored his outstretched hand and pushed past him to where Alcina lay. The prince had lifted her out of her half-crumpled position and laid her flat on the table as I had been. I crossed the room, heedless of the trail of blood I was leaving in my wake. Heedless of anything but her beautiful, still face. "Alcina," I said. My eyes burned. If she'd swallowed the apple...

I touched her skin, then recoiled when I saw the bloody smudge I left on her cheek. I didn't dare touch her lips with my dirty fingers. Instead, I leaned over, closed my eyes, and pressed my lips to hers.

Her mouth parted to me, still warm. I slipped my tongue against hers, then beneath, and — there. There it was.

The bite of the apple.

Carefully, I fished it out, then spat it on the floor and crushed it beneath the bloody heel of my boot.

"Snow White," breathed Alcina. "Snow White. You won."

"I did. Thanks to a little help," I said. A breeze tickled the back of my neck. For a moment I smiled through my tears. "Thank you, my friend," I whispered. My smile faded as my fears came rushing back. My father had been a terrible king, but he'd still been a king. Death by execution was the fate of anyone who stood against him, as all the history I'd read reminded me. For a brief, traitorous moment, I wondered if Prince Karl might be my way out. If *he'd* struck the deathblow it would be perfectly believable.

My stomach soured with shame as well as fear and disgust. What kind of queen would I be, if I built my rule on lies? If I began it by killing one who'd been my ally? What would Alcina think of me if I did such a thing?

Of course I could not blame Prince Karl for my crime. But if I wasn't careful, the choice might be taken from me. Others might choose to blame him rather than me if we were found like this together. "Who knows you're here?" I asked him.

"Only two of my most trusted men," he said. "They had their instructions if I didn't return."

I shook my head. "I still can't believe you came," I said through clenched teeth.

He shrugged and gave me a small smile. "Alcina said you needed my help, and that it might be a chance to stop the war."

His insouciance was irritating. He didn't seem to realize the position he was in. The position we were *all* in. I opened my mouth to tell him, but Alcina spoke up before I could say anything.

"I didn't think he would — would try to kill you," she said. She was perched on the table, looking away from the gory puddle a few feet away. "I should have realized. I'm sorry."

"I don't think any of us thought he would go that far," Prince Karl said. He glanced at the king's body, then back at the two of us. "What are you going to do?"

"I don't know." I went to put my head in my hands, but recoiled from the blood before I could touch my face. "I don't *know*."

Alcina laid a reassuring hand on my arm. "Breathe, Snow White." I took a breath and let it out slowly. "Good." She straightened, her gaze sweeping the room, her face becoming the expressionless mask she showed to others. "It would be better if no one knew the Prince was ever here."

"My two men are waiting for me outside of the castle," the prince said. "If I can get out without being seen, I can get back to my own people with no one the wiser."

"Why are you *here*, anyway?" I asked. "I mean, here in town? How did you get here so quickly?"

"The queen invited me two weeks ago," he said with a nod of his head.

I looked over at Alcina, who tilted her head to one side

and gave a tiny shrug. "I received word that your father was returning. I hoped I could arrange things to keep you safe and get you away from here."

I shook my head and resisted the urge to put my head in my hands again. "We'll talk about that later. For now," I swallowed hard. "I need to figure out what to tell... everyone. He was already spreading the rumor that you're a witch. If it gets out that I killed him..." I trailed off and swallowed again. She might be blamed as the instigator. As horrific as the image of my head rolling away from my body was, the idea of *hers*, her golden tresses stained with blood, was far worse.

There was a moment of heavy silence. "I think," Alcina said firmly, "that it would be best if everyone thinks he died in bed."

I opened my eyes and looked wordlessly at the corpse, pallid and mostly drained of blood, his head half off his neck, then back at Alcina.

She gave me a sardonic look. "I know. But there are things I can do with magic—"

"She nearly cut off his head!" Prince Karl exclaimed.

"I made everyone believe she was sick in bed for months!" Alcina shot back. "She wasn't even *here*! At least this time I have something to work with." A little of the horror faded from her eyes. "If Gregory can bring me another deer's heart there is a spell—"

"Do you really think we can hide the truth?" I interrupted her. My gaze swept over the blood-soaked room.

"With the help of my magic, yes," she said, sounding more confident. "I'll reattach his head. If we change him into clean clothes and put him in his bed, we can say that he died in his sleep."

"You cannot believe that will work," Prince Karl said.

I chuckled without any real humor. "If the alternative is to let everyone think that I murdered the king—or that *you* did—" I pointed at him, "then I'm willing to try."

"And how are you going to explain *this?*" Prince Karl said, gesturing at the blood-swamped stones.

I looked down at the sticky pool and felt an unexpected smile tug at my lips, even as determination straightened my shoulders. "Leave that to me." I undid my boots, leaving them behind as I crossed the room to the door, sock-footed and carefully avoiding the blood. "I have some experience with cleaning—" I swung the door open and stopped short as I came face to face with a man on the other side.

It was my father's general. The man he'd trusted most. I met his eyes and felt a shock of cold go through me. My fingertips went numb, and for a split second the walls seemed to close in.

"Your highness," he said.

"I—" I said, and stopped. The smell of blood was overpowering. My hands were covered in it in every way. Alcina's plan had kindled a small spark of hope, but it died as I stared into his implacable face.

"*Want help?*" came Wind's whisper. I swallowed hard. I didn't want to kill this man, but if it was him or me, or Alcina, or even Karl—

A gentle hand gripped my shoulder. "Boris," came my stepmother's voice, calm and even.

"Your Majesty," he said, and bowed to her.

"Were you listening?"

He met her gaze evenly. "Yes."

"You heard it all?"

"I did."

"What will you do?" The question was so quiet that she could have been asking about whether he would add milk to his tea.

He took in everything with those sharp eyes. The king's body, already cold. Prince Karl, child of our enemies. Me, blood drying on my clothes and skin. And Alcina, who stood tall and cool and unafraid.

"My wife has spoken to me of you," he said slowly, the words directed to Alcina. "You have ruled well in his stead. And you sent her a concoction that saved our daughter when she would have died." His back was like an iron rod, but he bent it nonetheless, going to one knee. "Long live the queen."

"Boris," she whispered, her eyes wide. "Thank you."

I stepped forward. "You must make sure Prince Karl is safely returned to his people without being seen. Can you do this?"

The general's eyes narrowed as they rested on the Prince. He looked away, and his gaze fell on the king's corpse. Something complicated flickered across the man's face: sorrow, I thought, but also relief. He seemed to age several years before my eyes. "I understand," he said at last. "I will do this."

I looked at Prince Karl, and he gave me a nod, accepting the necessity. "Good," I said. "Guard him with your life."

"I swear it," he said, and rose to lead the Prince safely away.

When they were gone, I turned to Alcina. "What do you need to make it look as though he died naturally?"

She was so ghostly pale that she seemed as though she might fade away into nothing in the thin light of the candles. I wanted to take her hands, to draw her into my arms and hold her. I dared not touch her, not when I was still drenched in blood. "The heart of a doe — no, a buck," she said. "And I must bring him to my workshop."

I considered. I could likely carry the king's body, especially as it was lighter now that it was missing so much blood. But it would be awkward and difficult, and I had other things to do. "Go to Gregory," I said. "Tell him to come and help me first, then send him to get that heart. I will take care of this room."

The queen stared at me for a long moment, then the corners of her lips curled into a small smile. "Yes, your Majesty," she said.

A chill ran up the back of my neck. "Don't call me that."

The sharp tone didn't seem to bother her. She merely inclined her head and said, "Very well, Snow White."

A different sort of frisson shivered through me. I gave myself a shake. "Go," I said. She nodded and disappeared through the doorway.

I would not have expected that my first night back at the palace would find me on my hands and knees, scrubbing blood-soaked stone. My prior experiences as a servant saved us: not only did I have the strength and the knowledge to clean the floor, I knew where to obtain the tools to do so — not just brushes and soap and buckets, but also used rags from the butchery. Then, too, I knew exactly where and how I could discard the water, rags, and even the bloodstained clothing without drawing suspicion.

It took hours. Hours of hauling dirty water away and dumping it out before refilling the buckets yet again. Hours of scrubbing, until my hands were raw, my body stiff, my shoulders aching. When I'd finished at last, only the faintest hint of a stain remained, and the small room stank of lye. I cleaned myself next, stripping down and scrubbing myself with fresh water and clean rags before changing into one of the 'ugly' dresses my stepmother had gifted me with... had it only been months ago?... it felt like years.

At last I dragged the heavy table to the center of the long room, until its shadow covered the subtle traces I hadn't been able to remove. Exhaustion dragged at me, and I nearly curled up on the floor then and there. But there was one more thing I knew I must do.

"Wind," I said aloud.

It was silent and still, then the faintest of whispers tickled my ear. *"I am here."*

"How?" I said. "I thought you couldn't leave the cottage. How did you come all the way to the castle?"

A soft breeze fluttered through my hair. *"I bound myself to you. You said you could bond with people. So I bonded with you for a little while."*

Closing my eyes, I smiled and tilted my head back, letting Wind stroke my cheeks. "Thank you," I said. "You saved me."

"That man was bad." There was something disapproving in the words, but still childish.

"Yes," I said.

Another brush of air over my cheek. *"I cannot stay,"* Wind said. *"I bonded with you, but it will not last. I must go back to the house."*

"You're leaving?" Tears gathered in the back of my throat. Wind fluttered around my face.

"Humans are too changeable. I understand now. The other Spirits couldn't help her. They couldn't change her, because humans change too much themselves. Every moment, you are different. The house stands still. You do not."

"How long?" I said.

"I am weakening every moment. As you change, so must I, and I cannot."

"Then—then go now," I said, swallowing back my tears and forcing a smile. "I don't want you to grow too weak." Lifting my hand, I felt the air winding between my fingers and skipping over my palm. It did feel lighter than I was used to. "I'll come back and visit you when I can."

A tiny puff of air against my cheek, as gentle as a butterfly's wings. *"Goodbye."*

"Goodbye, Wind. I will see you again," I promised.

There was no answer. The Spirit of Wind was already gone.

Somehow, I dragged myself to Alcina's quarters. Had I not known the castle intimately, especially the short cuts the servants used, I might not have made it. At that, it was only through sheer luck that I wasn't noticed, and through sheer stubbornness that I made it there without collapsing.

I ended up outside Alcina's secret room, barely remembering how I'd gotten there, and managed to lift my hand to rap on the wood. Even that simple action sent pain searing along my aching arm and through my shoulder.

There was a pause, then the door swung open. Alcina and Gregory were both inside, my father's corpse laid out on the long table. I peered at him in the lamplight. Somehow Alcina had reattached his head, leaving no trace of the wound behind. He was still pale and hollow cheeked, but at least he appeared whole.

My swordmaster frowned at me. "You're about to topple," he said, and Alcina's head snapped up.

"Put her in my bed," she ordered, and before I could object, I was lifted off my feet.

"I can walk," I protested, my words slurring, but the obstinate man ignored me. Moments later I was sinking into the mattress and being covered by smooth sheets. The gauze hanging around the bed brought back my dream. I squinted at it, but my eyelids were too heavy. They sank down despite myself, and pulled me into a deep, heavy sleep.

Chapter 14

I awoke feeling sore, yet comfortable. I shifted beneath the smooth sheets, yawned, and opened my eyes.

And froze.

Alcina was sleeping next to me, curled on her side. She was facing me, her honey colored hair escaping its loose braid, her eyes closed. I studied her, the way her lashes rested lightly against her cheek, the slow rise and fall of her chest as she breathed.

I would have liked nothing more than to have stayed there indefinitely. Unfortunately, my body would not allow it. Eventually I was forced to rise, moving as slowly as I could manage. Even so, she stirred and opened her eyes, looking adorably vague and sleepy.

"It's all right," I whispered. "Go back to sleep." She blinked at me, then closed her eyes. Her lips parted slightly.

Oh, how I wanted to kiss them.

I contented myself with a last look before taking myself off to handle my body's increasingly insistent demands.

I did not return immediately after. The sunlight was the pale gold of early afternoon. We'd slept through more than half the day, but I was awake now. Experimentally I flexed my hands and rolled my shoulders. They still ached, but I knew the pain would fade in a few more days. No one had come to awaken us, which meant that no one had yet raised the alarm about my father.

Someone, probably Gregory, had arranged food enough for both of us to be left in the sitting room. I devoured the simple meal of mostly bread and cheese, washing it down with water and savoring it more than I would have a feast of peacock and aged wine. A wry laugh escaped me when I saw the small jar of apple butter. It had once been a favorite of mine, but now I was irresistibly reminded of the apple I'd taken a bite out of just... was it only two days ago?

Eventually Alcina joined me, wandering in in her dressing gown, as disheveled as I'd ever seen her. I put together a plate for her and pressed it upon her as she settled into one of the chairs. "Good morning," I said. "Or good afternoon, as the case may be."

"Mm," she replied. She accepted the plate and began to nibble at a piece of bread thickly layered with apple butter. "Good afternoon."

I watched her, happiness unfurling in my chest. "Were you able to finish everything last night?"

"Yes," she mumbled around a mouthful before swallowing it. "It took some time and work, but I got him looking..." she dropped her eyes and put down the bread, "not normal, exactly, but at least not as though he'd had his throat cut."

"I'm sorry," I said.

She looked up, staring at me. "Do not apologize," she said. "He would have killed me. He would have killed both myself and the prince, had you not risked your life to fight him."

I turned my head away, the food sitting like a stone in my stomach. "I wish there had been another way."

"So do I," Alcina said. "If the fault lies with anyone, it is with me. I was the one who arranged the situation."

"You could not have known that my father would —"

"I should have," she sighed. I shook my head, and we were both silent for a time. My gaze drifted back to her. Finally she tore off a tiny piece of bread and ate it slowly, her eyes still distant.

"Well," I said, breaking the silence at last. "It turned out for the best. And at least this way I don't have to marry Prince Karl."

That drew her attention once more. Blinking, she said, "You're not going to marry him?"

"No," I said, frowning. "Surely there is no need to do so, now? You can continue to rule and I will continue to remain the crown princess. We will do our best to reconcile with our neighbors, of course—"

"If you don't marry him," Alcina interrupted, "*can* we fully reconcile?"

I clenched my jaw. "I'm not in love with him," I said, my voice carefully even. "Nor he with me."

"Your duty—"

"No!" I stood up, nearly sending the plate in my lap to the floor. I caught it and set it down on the table with a clunk, then turned away, trying to master my suddenly turbulent emotions. "I do not love him, Alcina! I want—I want to stay here with you!"

"Snow White," she said, her tone reasonable, "you must see that love doesn't matter for things such as this. And Prince Karl is a good man. In time, you will—"

"Never," I snapped. "I cannot love him. Not when my heart is already filled with someone else."

Silence hung over the room. I didn't dare look at Alcina.

"Who...?" It was such a quiet word, curiously flat.

I squeezed my eyes closed. The words pressed against my lips. I swallowed them back, but they rose up anyway. "Dearest," I said, "surely you know?"

The sharp gasp made me open my eyes at last. I turned to her despite myself. She was gazing at me, her face chalk-white, her blue eyes horrified. "But it was a dream," she whispered. "Is this—is this also a—?"

My heart pounded. The dream. It *had* been a shared dream.

The woman I'd kissed, the woman I'd held, the woman I'd *touched* hadn't been a figment of my imagination. She had been the true Alcina.

She loved me. She loved me as I loved her.

"Alcina," I gasped. I surged forward and pulled her against me. "I love you."

She shook in my arms. "It's not real," she whispered.

"It is." I stroked the back of her head and murmured against her temple. "I found a recipe for a potion in one of the books you left behind. The potion that lets one dream of their beloved." Her hair still smelled faintly of blood. "I dreamed of you. I told you about the books, the marital books—"

Her body went rigid against me. "This is another dream," she said. "It *must* be. Perhaps all of it is. It's all a drawn out nightmare, from the death of the king to—"

Swallowing hard, I loosened my embrace and sat back. "Is it a nightmare, then? Knowing that I love you?"

Her eyes were wet. "I can't—we *can't*," she said wretchedly. "I am your stepmother, Snow White!"

"You are far too young to be my mother," I said. Gently, I took both her hands in mine, letting my thumbs stroke over her knuckles. "Just two years separate us! You are barely old enough to be my sister!"

Her grip tightened on mine. "Nonetheless," she choked, "For me to love you, for you to love me, when I am your stepmother—"

"You never should have been." She stilled at that, her wet eyes lifting to meet mine. "My father never should have married you, a woman who did not want him, did not love him, yet felt she had no choice." Her grip on my hands tightened. "We found each other despite everything. If you did not feel the same, I would not ask anything of you. But you *do* feel the same as I. You want me," I said, more confidently than I felt. "You love me."

She did not deny it. "We cannot marry," she said thickly.

"I don't care." I leaned forward and brushed my lips against her cheek in an innocent gesture that nevertheless made my mouth tingle and my body burn. "I will not deny my feelings. If you ever were my stepmother, by any reckoning, you are no longer. You are free."

"Free," she sighed. Her shoulders loosened slightly, her head drooping. "If only it were so simple."

"It is. If you will allow me, I can take care of everything," I said. "Please, Alcina. Let me take care of you."

For a long moment, she did not move. I held my breath. Then, with the slow inevitability of a toppling tree, she slumped forward, further and further until her face was pressed to my shoulder. "I am so tired," she said, and I knew she didn't just mean from the long night before.

"Then let me," I said, folding her into my arms. Something new was growing in me, like a plant unfurling its leaves toward the sun. Alcina had been the one taking care of me for so long, helping me and guiding me and protecting me. It felt right that I would finally be able to do the same for her, now; no longer her charge, but her equal. "Let me protect you. Let me care for you. Ah, Alcina," I guided her head up until her lips were a breath away from mine. "Let me *love* you."

Her head dipped in slow nod, her voice almost too quiet to be heard. "Very well. If you — if you truly — "

I kissed her.

She tensed for a split second, and I held myself still, my lips soft and unmoving against hers. Then, all at once, she melted, going pliant under my hands and mouth. My breath caught, and I had to keep myself from grabbing her too tightly. Instead, I let my mouth linger teasingly against hers until she pressed forward with a small sound of impatience.

Heat flooded my veins, pooling in my stomach. She wavered between eagerness and hesitance, moving into me and then pulling back, shaking. I chased her, keeping my mouth soft on hers until she pressed against me again, a tender give and take. A tingling feeling ran up the back of my neck.

"S-Snow White," she said against my lips. I smiled, stroking up and down her back through her thin nightdress. She sighed and arched a little into my touch.

I thrilled at having her in my arms at last, warm and real. The dream had felt true, but this was better. Her heat, her skin, the weight of her body as I tugged her to rest against me once more; it was all so much more than I could have hoped for. But greater than that were the small imperfections: the rawness of my hands and stiff aching of my shoulders, the mingled faint smells of blood and sweat, the strong one of lye, the hungry gurgle of Alcina's stomach that made her flush and pull away, her hand going to her midsection.

I chuckled and tucked a strand of hair behind her ear. "You need to eat more," I said. "You must be famished."

Giving another shy nod she slipped out of my arms, settling primly next to me and picking up the plate she'd abandoned. I considered plucking a morsel and holding it to her lips, then discarded the idea. I could still feel the blood on my hands, though I'd scrubbed them thoroughly the night before.

Taking a bite, she chewed and swallowed. Her eyes slid to mine, then away. I watched with fascination and pleasure as color swept into her cheeks. She tore off another bit of bread. "What shall we do?" she asked.

I wanted to take her hands into mine once more and soothe her. Instead I moved until our sides were pressed together, letting the warmth of her body mingle with mine. "You left the king's body in bed?"

"Yes. In... our bed," she said with a little shudder. In addition to having her own quarters, of course, Alcina had been expected to share the king's bed when he was at home.

I frowned, my hands tightening into fists for a moment, before releasing them with a slow breath. He was gone by my hand. Any lingering resentment must be washed away by his blood.

"Will you let the servants find him?"

She nodded. "We have a little time. I gave orders that we were not to be disturbed. It will not be the first time he returned in the middle of the night and slept the day away."

"Are the servants still obeying you?"

"Mostly." She looked unseeingly down at her plate. "The rumors are nothing new, and your father took care not to let knowledge of your condition become widespread. He really did intend to have Prince Karl awaken you and then kill him."

"It wasn't your fault." I leaned harder against her. "Eat," I ordered, and she obediently took another bite. Satisfaction burst through me again, like a fresh berry on my tongue. I was the crown princess, in line to inherit the throne. It was past time I start acting like it. "After this, you will return to your shared chambers and alert the servants that the king passed away in his sleep." She nodded without a word. "I will leave the castle secretly tomorrow night and seek out Prince Karl. We will tell everyone that I was kidnapped and that he saved me and brought me home. That will help begin the reconciliation process between our countries."

"Are you *sure* you won't marry him?" Alcina asked.

"Quite sure," I said. "I won't leave you unless you truly wish me to. And I know you think it my duty to marry him, but my duty is to my people, first and foremost. You've worked hard to make sure I am beloved by my people. Now I will use that." I looked down at my own lap. "If you wish to leave, though, you can do so. The cottage is still there, and the spirits. You are free to return to them, if that is what you want."

She went silent, hardly even seeming to breathe. "Free," she said again. "Free to choose."

"Yes," I said, my heart sinking like a stone. I loved her and she loved me, but would it be enough?

She turned her blue eyes upon me, studying me. "Many times I wished that I could return to my cottage," she said, her voice filling the silence with the clarity of small bells. "But now I find that—that it isn't what I want, after all."

"Alcina," I breathed, my eyes stinging.

"I don't know what we shall do," she said, "but I will stay by your side until the end."

I did not expect the 'discovery' of my father's corpse to go smoothly. I stayed in Alcina's private chambers, ready to come out and take charge should it become necessary. The plan was for me to hide away until Prince Karl could 'rescue' me. But, plan or no plan, I would have no compunction about revealing myself if Alcina was in danger. I had impressed upon Gregory in the strongest possible terms that if it looked as though the servants didn't believe Alcina, or if they were prepared to turn on her, that he must get me *at once*.

I therefore waited nervously for over an hour, jumping at the slightest sound, convinced that Alcina would be dragged away and killed before I could do anything to stop it.

Finally, late in the afternoon, I heard the door to the outer chambers open and close. My head snapped up from the book I hadn't been able to concentrate on.

When Alcina herself appeared in the doorway, rather than Gregory, relief soared through me.

"You're all right," I said, and she paused, her eyes sweeping over my face and my hands, which I had gripped together in front of me.

"Yes," she said. "Did you think I would not be?"

"You're the one who took such pains to convince everyone you were a witch," I said, trying for dry and ending up at petulant. "And my father had you thrown in the dungeon." I still felt a spike of fury at that, despite the fact that I had inarguably had my revenge. "It must have been terribly suspicious to show up two mornings later claiming that he'd died in his sleep."

"It was not as bad as you think," Alcina said with a calm that would have been infuriating if it were not so familiar. It was the same face she showed the world, impassive and untouchable, but I knew how soft and vulnerable she was beneath the mask. "Your father only brought a handful of men with him to the cottage, all highly trusted and discreet, and his general is quite brilliant. He's handled the situation beautifully. Gregory, too, helped a great deal. And," she hesitated, then went on, "apparently the servants have some loyalty to me, despite the fact that I never sought it."

I laughed helplessly at that. Of course my beloved had no idea of the impact she had on other people. She'd tried to hold herself aloof, never accounting for the small kindnesses and gestures of appreciation she was always making. Simple words of gratitude, quietly ensuring that servants who were ill had time to recover, that those with families had time to spend with them. For every word of malicious gossip, there had been one of praise for the queen. Not for her warmth, perhaps, but for her fairness, her thoughtfulness, and her deliberate attempts to see that people had what they most needed.

The only 'unfairness' she'd ever shown had been toward me, and the people closest to me had seen the way that I'd blossomed and thrived. And if I held no grudge against the woman who was ostensibly making my life hell, why should they?

"So the servants accepted your account?"

"Apparently so," she said. "As far as the vast majority of the kingdom is concerned, you are still missing, and the king passed away naturally in the night. There is still a great deal of concern about you, but it seems that most are relieved that at least I am here to rule."

I nodded. "I will leave at full dark tonight and return as soon as I can."

"Come and eat first," she said.

"Food?" I asked, pathetic and hopeful.

Her lips quirked up into a smile. "I left it in the front chamber."

"You're wonderful," I said fervently, and watched in fascination as her cheeks flushed a dark pink that spread across her face until even her forehead was stained with color.

"Flatterer," she managed, her voice intriguingly choked.

"It's only flattery if you don't mean it," I said with a wicked grin. I liked this new thing between us, where I could tease her and make her blush. She turned away, leading the way into the other room.

Seeing Prince Karl again was very odd. The last time we'd seen each other I'd been covered in blood and bending over my father's corpse. Now I wore the most faded and worn clothes I could find, a frayed piece of cloth covering my hair and dirt smeared on my cheeks. I kept my head down and my shoulders hunched as I slipped through the inn and past the Prince's guards. They didn't even challenge me, not as long as I had a coal scuttle in my hands.

If I ever wished to assassinate a foreign member of the royalty, I reflected, it would be all too easy. Luckily for Prince Karl, that was the opposite of what I wished. I needed the young man alive and well for what was to come next.

He was frowning over a map when I entered, and ignored my presence until I addressed him. Then his head snapped up, his affronted expression melting into a satisfyingly shocked one when he realized who I was. "*Snow White?*"

"Hush!" I glanced warily at the door, but no one burst into the room, a fact which was simultaneously an irritation and a relief.

"Your guards need to be better trained," I said, keeping my voice low. "What if I was an assassin?"

Blinking, the prince glanced at the door, then back at me. He opened his mouth as though to argue, but closed it again without speaking, his lips curling into a rueful grin. Finally he said, "Apparently they do. What are you doing here?"

"You're going to 'rescue' me and return me to my bereaved stepmother."

"Am I?"

"You are," I said firmly.

"I see." His smile faded. "And after I return you to your home?"

I set my jaw. "I know you want us to marry. You and Alcina both."

"It's less a matter of what I want—" he began.

"It's what you think we *should* do, then," I said. "You believe it is our duty to marry. But if I marry you, I will be forced to leave my kingdom, my people, and," I stopped, catching back the words 'my love'.

He gave me a knowing look that slowly turned thoughtful. "You have no brothers or sisters."

"No."

"I do," he said. I nodded, remembering the family trees

I'd been forced to memorize. His gaze went distant before drifting down to the map in front of him. "What if I were to marry you and live here?"

"Here? But who would rule—" I stopped. "One of your brothers?"

"We've all been trained for it. Any of them could step into my place."

I stared at him. "You would do that?"

His lips tightened, his gaze fixed unseeingly on the map. "You do not love me, nor I you."

"No," I said again.

"So if we were to be married," he paused delicately, "you would not object if I did not, that is…"

"*If* we were ever married, I would prefer you touch me as little as possible," I said bluntly. "I would certainly not object to you finding joy in the arms of another. Provided you did not object if I did the same."

He *blushed*. A surge of pleased affection warmed my heart, and I thought again, that perhaps if things had been different, he would have been someone I could have fallen in love with.

Or perhaps not. I could not imagine loving anyone as I did Alcina. I swallowed and went on, "But won't your family take issue with it, if you marry me and leave your own kingdom behind? That is not the way it's generally done."

"I have four brothers," he said, his tone a little dry. "And I know my mother would like to see me happy," he added, his voice softening. "If we made it a condition of peace between our realms, they might accept it. They are as tired of the constant wars as your people are."

"*Would* you be happy?" I could not imagine leaving my kingdom and my people behind to rule over strangers. It was one thing to hide in a cottage in the woods for a time. It was quite another to marry into a different family and move to another place entirely.

"I don't know," he said, and blew out a breath. "But I think I might. If I could be with," the flush on his cheeks darkened again, "the person I love, it would be — it would be worth it."

I nodded, thinking of Alcina. If the only way she and I could be together was to abandon my own kingdom, that would change things. Would I choose her over my people? No, I knew I wouldn't. But if I had a sibling ready and able to take over and rule in my stead? If being with her didn't necessitate abandoning my own responsibilities?

That would be a bargain I could accept, I thought. Especially if it was the only way she and I could be together. Offering such an opportunity to my friend was no hardship, particularly as it would neatly dovetail with my own plans. And looking to the future, it would keep my people from demanding that I marry someone else. Alcina and I could never officially be married; my father's selfishness had seen to that.

"If you think your family would agree to it," I said, "it would make things a great deal easier for me." He nodded, his eyes going distant again. I wondered who he was imagining, to make him smile so. I supposed I would meet them eventually, if we were to be wedded. "First things first," I broke into his reverie. "We need to have you 'rescue' me and return with me to the castle."

He straightened, his attention drawn back to me. "Yes, your highness," he said with a flourishing bow.

I rolled my eyes, making him laugh.

Chapter 15

The news spread faster than I could have imagined. After some discussion, the Prince and I decided to ride separately, surrounded by his guards. We sent messengers ahead to spread word of my rescue and return, and by the time we were halfway home, the streets were lined with cheering people. I was grateful it was winter, or we would no doubt have been pelted with flowers. Even as it was, people tossed ribbons and feathers and other frivolous things until we were surrounded by a colorful rain.

It was gratifying, and also embarrassing. Prince Karl handled it with equanimity, smiling and waving, catching a beautifully embroidered handkerchief before it could hit him in the face and brushing his lips across it before offering it to me. I met his eyes, carefully not rolling mine, and accepted it. The crowd was delighted.

Somehow we made it through the exhausting day that followed. The best moment was when Alcina came out to meet us at the castle entrance, dressed in her finest clothing. Her normally impassive affect was absent; instead she was smiling, *beaming* as we approached. I dismounted and ran to grasp her outstretched hands, wishing I could do more. Wishing I could take her in my arms and claim her lips.

Later, I promised myself.

First, there was a feast that the kitchen had to throw together with almost no warning (I apologized to the cook profusely), rooms and beds to be prepared for the unexpected guests, and I had to accept the well-wishes of countless people, from the lowest maid to the highest noble.

In the end, it wasn't until late that I was able to slide into my own bed. I had thought that I would fall asleep at once, but the sight of the tapestry across from me brought back the helplessness I'd felt but a few days ago, and I found myself unable to settle.

Alcina didn't seem surprised when she opened her door to me, candle in hand.

"Did I wake you?" I asked guiltily, but she shook her head.

"No, I was sitting up reading," she admitted. "Come in."

I followed her gratefully, but paused when we reached her inner chamber. She slid into bed, then turned and looked at me inquiringly. Swallowing, I climbed in next to her and slid an arm around her waist and pressed close.

Her hand drifted over to tuck a strand of hair behind my ear. "Snow White," she murmured.

"Alcina," I whispered. "I missed you."

"You weren't gone for very long," she said sardonically.

I smiled. "Any length of time without you is too long."

She breathed a laugh and stroked my cheek. I turned my head and brushed my lips against her fingers. "You are," she said, her breath catching, "you are ridiculous."

"You are beautiful."

"Ah," she laughed again, shaking her head. "Ridiculous!"

I wrapped my hand around hers and tugged it until I could press my lips against her wrist, feeling her pulse fluttering against my skin. Her laughter stopped with a gasp. "S-Snow White."

"Alcina," I begged, "can I?"

Her eyes went wide, darkening. She caught her lower lip between her teeth. My attention narrowed in on it so tightly that I almost missed the moment when she gave a nod. It wasn't until her trembling fingers brushed over my lips, leaving them tingling from that bare touch, that I realized that she'd given me permission.

For a moment I was paralyzed, my senses swamped with need. I forced myself to move slowly, gently, trailing my fingers over the shell of her ear, just as I'd done in our shared dream.

She shivered. "I can't believe this is real," she whispered. "I can't—I shouldn't have this."

"I want to give it to you," I said fiercely, but strove to keep my touch light. She shivered again, her fingers gripping the fabric of my nightdress.

"Can I," she said, breathless, then stopped.

"Whatever you want," I said, following the words with a kiss to the side of her neck. "Anything you want."

"I want to touch you," she burst out.

I couldn't have stopped myself from smiling even if I'd wanted to. "That's not a hardship, Alcina."

She gave her head a little shake. "Wretched girl. How I love you," she gasped, and kissed me.

To feel her desire at last, to know that her hunger matched mine, settled something in my heart and made my body burn anew. "*Your* wretched girl."

An inarticulate sound came from her throat, but whether it indicated frustration or need or something else I couldn't tell. Nor did she give me an opportunity to figure it out. She fell on me like she'd been starving. Her kisses were clumsy but passionate, pressed to my cheeks, my forehead, my ears, my neck.

It was my turn to gasp, overwhelmed. "Yes, oh, darling—" She made another sound, higher than the first, and scraped her teeth against my shoulder, not hard enough to hurt, but enough to send a shudder racing through me. I tried to touch her in turn, but she caught my wrists and pressed them back into the bed.

"Let me," she said. "Let me. It's my turn."

"If that is your wish," I said, and she squeezed my wrists before releasing them.

"It is. Let me. You are," her voice took on a rueful note, "you are far too distracting."

Pleasure washed through me at her admission, so much more than mere carnal satisfaction.

"Oh, you smug thing," she panted, and kissed me again, her tongue delightfully demanding.

It was harder than I would have guessed, holding myself back. I wanted to make her writhe again. Wanted her skin under my hands, my mouth. But she was right. It *was* her turn.

So I let her tug my nightdress off and over my head but did not demand she remove hers in turn. I let her trace over my skin, her hands sweet and hot, awakening my body in ways I'd never experienced, even with the help of the book and the True Magic of the dream.

It was different when it was her hands on me. It was different when it was *real*.

She kissed her way down my neck, lingering lightly in the hollow of my throat and sending strange, wonderful chills down my scalp and the back of my neck. Her right hand found my left breast, her thumb tracing a slow spiral inward.

"So soft," she groaned, fingers skating over the skin of the underside of my breast before finding their exploratory way to my nipple. A cry caught in my throat as she pinched it, not quite hard enough to hurt, but enough to focus my attention entirely on the sensation. "Yes," she hissed. My back bowed into an arch as she rolled my peaking nipple between two fingers. "Is it good?" There was a dip in her voice, a moment of hesitation before the last word.

"*Yes*," I gasped.

"So I should keep doing this?" Now there was a smile in her voice.

"And you call *me* smug," I said. "It's good," I admitted, but shifted impatiently under her hand. "I—I—will you—"

"Hm?" she leaned down and *licked* me, her hot, slick tongue painting a circle over my puckered, sensitive skin.

My head tossed back, my body arching again. Heat surged up into my stomach and burned down between my legs.

"Please," I whimpered with frustration.

She stilled, her mouth still on me, then lifted her head. "What is it? What am I doing wrong?" Her teasing smile was gone, her brows drawn together in worry.

I shifted and turned, willing her to understand. She only watched my face, until finally, desperate, I mumbled, "My other nipple."

"Oh," she said, her forehead smoothing. "I *see*." Leaning down, she breathed across my right nipple, not quite touching it with those tempting, teasing lips.

"Please," I said again. I could feel the way the word affected her in the rush of her breath, the tremble in her body.

"Anything," she whispered. "Anything it's within my power to give is yours."

"You." The word was out without thought or hesitation. "You." Some part of me cried out at that, knowing I wouldn't abandon my people even for her, but the words kept spilling out of me anyway. "I would live with you in this castle or in your cottage in the woods. I would move to another country if that was your desire, as long as you came with me. You are all I want. You are everything I want."

"Where," she demanded, dropping her head against my skin, "where did you learn to speak like this?"

"It is only the truth," I told her, and she shook her head, her hair trailing against me ticklishly.

"You," she said, but didn't finish the thought. Or perhaps that was the complete thought in itself, just 'You' and nothing more. At last, her lips found my other nipple. I squirmed, jolts of liquid lightning coursing down to strike at the parting of my legs. Mindlessly, I pushed away my underclothes, my thighs spreading open of their own accord beneath the thin sheet, the only thing left between us. I reached to push it down the rest of the way, but Alcina stopped me, catching my wrist and pressing it back against the bed. I stared up at her. Her cheeks were flushed, her eyes warm, but with a lurking uncertainty behind them still.

"It's alright," I whispered.

She nodded, but dropped her eyes to my chest, the corners of her lips tightening. I recognized the look, one she wore in court when dealing with particularly intransigent lords.

"Alcina?"

Giving her head a little shake, she lay one hand on the sheet over my stomach, then slid it down over the fabric. I squealed as she pressed down between my legs, helplessly grinding up into her touch, blindly seeking more.

I would have rubbed myself raw, but she gave a stuttering little gasp, drawing my attention away from my own body for a moment. Her eyes fluttered shut, her hand still pressing hard against the linen. I opened my mouth to speak again, but before I could do so, her eyes opened. Reaching down, in a single smooth movement she drew the sheet the rest of the way off.

Cool air washed over my heated skin. I was exposed, naked, utterly vulnerable and powerless against this woman. It was terrifying and exhilarating in equal measure.

Sitting up, she just looked at me for a long moment. Her gaze raked down my face, my body. There was more than just lust in her eyes. She stared at me with a fascination, an *awe* that brought a different kind of heat to my cheeks and made me want to tear my gaze away.

Instead I forced myself to meet her eyes. I waited, my body throbbing and shaking.

"Do you want," she began, then stopped.

"Anything," I said. She had all of my trust. All of my love.

It took only a moment for her to climb over me, settling between my legs. My knees folded outward without a conscious thought on my part, the petals of a flower unfurling, a butterfly's wings spreading wide for the first time, natural and inevitable.

Slowly, she lowered her head and pressed a kiss to the burning place at the join of my legs.

"Yes," the words fell from my lips without conscious volition, "yes, Alcina, yes, yes, yes."

I could see the edge of her lips curving — smug, I thought again, but justifiably so — before she breathed a puff of air across my too-hot skin. Her lips parted.

Perhaps I should have demurred. In the dream she'd been so hesitant, so disgusted by the idea of this act. Now she moved slowly but steadily, her tongue *finally* flicking out and stroking over that spot where I yearned to be touched. "*Alcina!*" I cried.

Her hands tightened on my thighs. She surged forward like the tide, all hesitation abruptly washed away. Her tongue swept up, leaving a spike of sensation in its wake. I sucked in air, weakness weighing down my limbs. My legs spread even wider, as wide as they would go. She hummed against me, taking advantage of my exposure to tease and explore in equal measure. The more I writhed and shuddered, the more eager she became, her mouth on me insistent and inescapable.

Then she wriggled around, not quite lifting her head, and reached up to grab a pillow. Shoving it under her chest, she propped herself up and freed her hands to — oh — slide up and find my nipples again. I jolted as she rolled them between thumb and forefinger, both at once, even as her tongue stayed busy between my legs. New waves of delicious sensation surged through me, echoing under her tongue.

A sudden thread of clarity wound beneath the passion swamping my mind. She was doing to me exactly everything I'd done to her. In this, I'd been *her* teacher. The idea ignited me anew, turning my already burning body molten.

"Ah, ah, *ah*—" I couldn't form words anymore, could only arch and press up into that exquisite touch. Alcina's mouth never stopped, even as I pulled away from her, then pushed back up again and again, the waves rising to an inexorable crest. More sounds spilled from me, incoherent and wild.

She didn't stop.

The wave crashed.

She didn't stop.

I shook violently, my hips drawing away and lifting again. She let me pull back, her mouth all the more enthusiastic when my body shoved up again. I hung on the edge of a knife, between too much and not quite enough. Tears sprang to my eyes, squeezed out from between my tightly-shut eyelids.

Her touch gentled, drew back. My body followed it. Her fingers left my nipples and found their way between my legs, one to tease and rub at that insatiable place, the other thrusting inside.

I rode her hands, grinding against one with abandon, clenching around the other wantonly.

The wave rose again like the tide returning. I let it lift me up, carrying me higher and still higher, until, with the suddenness of a thunderclap, it became too much.

Shoving one hand between my pulsing, tingling flesh and her touch, I cupped it protectively over myself and pleaded, "No more, no more, I can't—"

Lifting her head, she wiped the back of one arm over her mouth. It was such a human gesture, so far from the restrained and refined queen she presented to the rest of the world, that it pulled a weak laugh from me. She gave me a coy look and pressed her hand atop mine where I shielded myself, pushing my fingers down onto my aching, overstimulated skin. I choked on a cry, twisting up and then away.

She released me with a huff of laughter, sliding up next to me and winding one arm around my waist. I buried my face in her shoulder, my body still shivering as smaller swells rocked through me, echoes of the powerful climax.

For a long moment I lay limp, my panting breath loud in the silent room. Then I reached for her, my hands clumsy as I fumbled down her body, glancing awkwardly off her skin. "Alcina," I said, half-sighing, half-pleading.

"It's all right," she said. "Relax."

"I want to —"

"Don't worry," she said. "We have time."

"But I *want* to," I whined.

"Here." Taking my hand, she pulled it gently between her thighs. She was wet there, slippery and hot. Still gripping my hand, she rocked into it, rubbing against my touch. I tried to help, but she snapped, "Be still." So I nodded and let her use me, wondering if I could convince her to do it again someday, to use my body and rub herself against my fingers, or my thigh, or any part of me, really. The idea brought back that fluttering feeling in my stomach. I *wanted* to be used. I wanted her to do it when I wasn't too weak to appreciate it. Perhaps she could bind me, so that I couldn't touch myself, and then tease me until —

Her movements and quiet sounds rose to a crescendo. She pulsed and clenched against my hand. Satisfaction flooded me. We *would* do this again. Again and again. I would *make* it happen.

She pushed my hand away and wrapped her arms around me. "Snow White," she said into my tangled, sweaty hair. Her voice shook.

"Alcina." I forced myself to pull back, to meet her eyes,

taken aback by her sudden shift of mood. Her pupils were wide, turning the ring of blue around them dark.

"Thank you," she breathed.

I laughed again. "No need for that, after all we both—" I began, but she interrupted me.

"No, not that." She shook her head, her golden hair catching the light and trailing over her pale shoulders. "I didn't—I didn't *know*," she said, the words somehow agonized. "I never *knew*."

I opened my mouth to respond, but nothing came out. I didn't know what to say.

She clutched at me, pulling me hard against her, her lips pressed to my shoulder. "I would never have known," she mumbled into my skin.

My clean hand moved without conscious thought, combing through her hair, gently stroking the back of her head. My still-sticky hand wound around her, settling against the small of her back. "Known?" I said, my voice just barely above a whisper this time.

She shook her head a little, her mouth sliding against my skin. When she lifted her head she was smiling, though the rims of her eyes were red. "Love."

The word rocked through me, making me clutch at her in turn. She deserved love as few I had ever known, to love and to be loved, to take pleasure in loving and to give pleasure as well.

"Snow White," she said, catching my lips in a long, sweet kiss. When we parted at last, she whispered for my ear alone, gifting me with her True name.

Arranging things with Prince Karl's family was both easier and more difficult than I'd expected. They were willing enough to let him abdicate in favor of his brother, an ambitious young man who apparently had high hopes and many plans for the future of his kingdom. Prince Karl, more easygoing (and perhaps a little lazy) quietly admitted to me that he was just as glad not to have the responsibility, and that his brother would make a good king.

But working out the details took nearly a year of negotiations. A year of diplomats traveling back and forth. A year of traveling back and forth ourselves, to discuss matters too delicate to leave to our representatives.

It could have been worse. Alcina still ruled in name, and would until I was married. In truth, we shared the responsibilities, taking turns holding court in the afternoons, arguing about the proper way to handle major and minor issues, and loving, loving, loving each other.

We met Prince Karl's beloved, Noel, for the first time during the negotiations. He was a wiry, clever young man. His eyes and hair were as black as mine, though his skin was dark as well, darker even than the farmers who spent long days toiling in the sun. Despite this, Alcina thought he looked a bit like me. I found it amusing, as I'd always thought that Prince Karl resembled Alcina, though lacking the elements, physical and otherwise, that made her irresistible. Noel was both a commoner and male, which explained why the two couldn't simply be married. Even if his country had allowed marriages between men, a marriage so far below his station would never have been countenanced.

One day, after many hours of discussions and negotiations, Prince Karl invited me to spar. I gladly accepted. We fought to a draw, and afterwards sat side by side in the shade of the palace wall, drinking water and talking quietly.

"I made him my personal manservant," Prince Karl confided to me. "But it was a mistake. He rose through the ranks of the servants too quickly, and the rest of the staff were jealous. They treat him very badly." His lips twisted into an unhappy frown. "The more I tried to stop it, the worse it got."

I nodded. Having worked with the servants in my own palace, I'd seen how easily one person could earn the enmity of the rest, especially if it was believed that they'd gained some special favor that they didn't deserve. Alcina had always been very careful not to play favorites, and I'd learned to follow her example, or to give a clear explanation if someone did merit special treatment. "I believe that can be avoided when you both move here permanently," I said. "There will be some natural distrust as you are both outsiders, but since he will already have a high position going in, there will be less envy. I have a few ideas for ways you can smooth the transition, too. Small gifts for the staff, that sort of thing."

"Bribery?" he asked, sounding amused.

"Why not?" I countered.

He took another sip of his water. I noted that despite his smile, his shoulders were still tight.

"It will be alright," I said, knocking my arm against his just enough to jostle him and make him spill water down his chin.

Glaring at me, he wiped his face and said, "You're very sure."

I shrugged. "I have worked more closely with my servants than you ever have with yours, I'll wager."

"Then the rumors are true?" His eyes widened. "The queen forced you to do servant's work?"

"She never forced me to do anything," I snapped. "Everything I did, I did by choice."

He lifted his hand placatingly. "I meant no offense."

"No," I said, drawing a deep breath, "I am not offended, merely tired of such accusations being thrown at the queen.

Even if she wanted it that way."

"Wanted it...?" He tilted his head inquiringly. I gave him a slight smile.

"It's a long story," I said, and finished the last of my water. "Someday I'll tell you all about it." I glanced at the sky and sighed. "I don't think we have time for another round."

"No," he agreed, standing and offering me a hand. I eyed it for a moment before taking it and hauling myself to my feet.

Noel stepped forward from the sidelines with a cloth for the Prince, who accepted it with a smile and a quiet, "Thank you." To my surprise, the young man offered me one as well.

"Thank you," I echoed, meeting his eyes. He nodded and bowed, his manner exceedingly correct. I wondered how he and Prince Karl had met; how they had fallen in love. Perhaps we could trade stories after we were married.

Epilogue

More than a year.

It had been more than a year, nearly a year and a half all-told, since I'd left the cottage.

Alcina had gone before me, just after Prince Karl and I were 'wed', leaving me solely in charge of the kingdom. Well, not 'solely', since my husband now ruled at my side as my consort.

"The people need to see you ruling without me," she said when I objected—I hated when we had to be separated. "They need to know that you're no longer a child, and that you can handle the duties of the queen without my help. And they need to learn to trust Karl, so that you can eventually take turns."

I groused, but I knew she was right. I also knew I would miss her terribly. As far as my people knew, she'd gone into 'seclusion' after my marriage and her abdication.

"Take this with you," I said, unclasping the locket she'd given me. "So they will know it's you."

She hesitated, then accepted it with a bemused smile. "You never opened it?"

I shook my head, a little offended. "I promised."

Ducking her head shyly as she never did in public, she flicked open a hidden catch. On the left side of the locket was a midnight-black curl of hair. The right side contained a tiny portrait...of me.

"I inherited the locket from Frea," Alcina admitted. "She said it was a gift from a grateful woman who had nothing else to give. Frea had saved it in case she ever needed to sell it. It was empty when I first began wearing it." Her lips twisted into a grimace. "Your father gave me a miniature portrait of himself to put in it. But I—I secretly took it out and replaced it with yours."

"When?" I breathed.

"The day you met Prince Karl." She stroked one finger over the dark lock of hair. "You sparred with him. The two of you got along better than I'd hoped. And I knew I should be happy for it, but," she shook her head. "It hurt," she whispered. "Knowing I would lose you to him. I commissioned the miniature portrait in secret. Snipping the strand of hair was easy."

"It was?"

"I just said that it was too long."

As she spoke, the memory returned to me. She'd insisted on getting her embroidery scissors and trimming the lock herself. "I never guessed that you had an ulterior motive."

"I hardly admitted it even to myself. It was all right to carry your image and a lock of your hair with me, I told myself, because you were my stepdaughter. But in my heart I knew it was a lie. I was beginning to love you in a different way, much to my shame."

"*Alcina*," I said, and kissed her, the locket dangling from her fingers, forgotten.

The nights were the worst, far too lonely without her at my side (or in my arms). But between the burdens of leadership and getting my consort (and his beloved) settled in, the time did not weigh so heavily as I'd feared it would. I will admit to a slight stab of envy when I went to bed each night exhausted and lonely, knowing that Karl was snugly curled up with his beloved. But I awoke each morning with the knowledge that I was one day closer to seeing her again.

Finally the day arrived. This would be only a short trip. Prince Karl would be in charge, secretly but ably assisted by Noel. I dressed in my oldest and most nondescript clothing, covered my hair with a scarf and smeared my face with dirt, packed a few things into my saddlebags, and left, Gregory and a few of my most trusted guards my only escort.

The day was pleasant. It had been winter when I'd been carried away from the cottage. Now it was summer, the world grown hot and green. We made our way through the towns at a decent pace, but it was still several hours before we entered the forest, my swordmaster leading the way. The air was cooler and damper beneath the trees, and I gratefully drew in deep lungfuls.

My heart beat hard as I finally began to recognize my surroundings. We'd had to dismount and walk, much to the dismay of some of my companions. I continued forward, though, driven almost as much by my desire to return to the cottage as my desire to see Alcina.

In the end I was almost running, finding my way through familiar paths between the trees. Past where I'd found the herb that had let me share the dream with Alcina. Past Frea's grave. Past the cool, fresh stream that ran down from the mountains. Finally, finally, the trees parted and revealed the clearing. Joy surged through me. The windowless cottage still stood, the garden on the side well-tended and healthy. And in the doorway stood Alcina herself, her arms open. I dropped the reins and ran to her.

It would only be a short visit, no more than a week, and then we would both be returning to the castle together. But as Wind stirred my hair and laughed in my ear, I knew we would come here again as often as we could, to live in our cottage in the woods. I would finally cook a meal for Alcina, using the spices and supplies I'd brought with me in my horse's saddlebags. We would bathe together at last, in water heated by the Spirit of Warmth. She would read the new romantic stories I'd brought, her head in my lap. And the two of us would study the marital books together, blushing yet eager. We couldn't stay here forever, but we didn't need to. It would be here for us, waiting, for as long as we needed it.

"*Welcome*," whispered the Spirit of Wind. "*Welcome home.*"

About the Author

When it comes to fusing elaborate high fantasy with steamy queer romance, no one does it better than five-time Hugo Finalist **Laura Weyr**! Her first full-length novel, *The Eighth Key*, won the 2021 Rainbow Award for Best Gay Fantasy Romance. Laura lives in sunny California with her husband, daughter, and cat. Stay tuned for more from this talented author!

~

The lifeblood of every author is audience feedback. Please consider leaving a review (of whatever length) on Amazon, GoodReads, or your favorite platform.

About the Publisher

Founded in 2019 by Galactic Journey's Gideon Marcus, **Journey Press** publishes the best science fiction, current and classic, with an emphasis on the unusual and the diverse. We also partner with other small presses to offer exciting titles we know you'll like!

Also available from Journey Press:

The Eighth Key by **Laura Weyr**
A steamy fantasy romance

The magic is gone…or is it?

Lucian is a jaded flirt and professional bard who knows all the old songs about sorcery. When he meets Corwin, a shy mage who can still use magic despite the Drought, Lucian finds his desire growing with each passing day—not just for answers, but for Corwin himself.

At First Contact by **Janice L. Newman**
The Fantastical Romances You've Been Craving

Hugo Finalist Janice L. Newman presents a touching trio of romances in a speculative vein. From the edge of space, to the shadows of the paranormal, to the marvels of the mystic, these stories show love can be found even in the most unlikely settings.

Sibyl Sue Blue by Rosel George Brown
The Original Woman Space Detective

Who she is: Sibyl Sue Blue, single mom, under-cover detective, and damn good at her job.

What she wants: to solve the mysterious benzale murders, prevent more teenage deaths, and maybe find her long-lost husband.

How she'll get it: seduce a millionaire, catch a ride on his spaceship, and crack the case at the edge of the known galaxy.

By Your Side: The First 100 Years of Yuri Anime and Manga by Erica Friedman
The Untold Story of Lesbian Love in Japanese Anime and Comics

Two decades in the making, By Your Side is a collection of essays, scholarly and approachable, by the Western Hemisphere's authority on the subject. This landmark work should be in the library of any fan of anime, manga, lesbian relationships in media–or any combination of the three!

Printed in the USA
CPSIA information can be obtained
at www.ICGtesting.com
LVHW090406101123
763531LV00007B/86